Mary-Kate and Ashley

Sweet 16

NEVER BEEN KISSED

By Emma Harrison

HarperEntertainment
An Imprint of HarperCollinsPublishers

A PARACHUTE PRESS BOOK

A PARACHUTE PRESS BOOK

Parachute Publishing, L.L.C.
156 Fifth Avenue, Suite 302
New York, NY 10010

Published by
📓HarperEntertainment
An Imprint of HarperCollins*Publishers*
10 East 53rd Street, New York, NY 10022-5299

SWEET 16 books are created and produced by Parachute Press, L.L.C., in
cooperation with Dualstar Publications, a division of Dualstar Entertainment
Group, Inc., published by HarperEntertainment, an imprint of HarperCollins
Publishers.

ISBN 0-06-009209-2

HarperCollins®, 📓®, and HarperEntertainment™ are trademarks of HarperCollins
Publishers Inc.

First printing: April 2002

Printed in the United States of America

Visit HarperEntertainment on the World Wide Web at
www.harpercollins.com

10 9 8 7 6 5 4 3 2 1

chapter one

"Ashley? Are you ready yet?" I called out, barely able to hide the excitement in my voice.

"Just give me a couple of minutes!" my sister, Ashley, answered from the dressing room next to mine.

I stared at myself in the mirror. The store dressing room was completely littered with clothes, but I'd found the perfect outfit at last. I couldn't stop smiling. "Do I look great or what?" I asked myself.

The answer was yes.

The knit top I chose brought out my blue eyes and looked killer with the short denim shorts. It was perfect for our sweet sixteen party.

"Ashley, hurry up!" I called. "I'm dying to see what you think of this outfit!"

"I've just got a few more dresses to try," Ashley called back. I rolled my eyes and sat down to wait on the little bench in my dressing room, pushing the pile of clothes aside. *Our party is going to be sooo great,* I thought. I let my mind wander off. . . .

All of our girlfriends are hanging out on the beach and it's a sunny, breezy day. There's a DJ spinning in the sand while a bunch of people dance to the latest songs. A few people swim in the waves. The rest of the crowd watches as Ashley and I rule in a volleyball tournament. Dad mans the barbecue while Mom snaps pictures of our friends.

We hang out on the beach until the stars come out, dancing to our favorite hits next to a big bonfire. Our cake is huge and has tons of candles on it. All our friends gather around to sing to us. Everyone agrees that it's the most fantastic sweet sixteen they've ever been to.

And, of course, there's a monster pile of presents waiting for us when it's all over. Can't forget about the presents. . . .

"Almost ready, Mary-Kate." Ashley's voice snapped me out of my thoughts. The beach and the party all melted away. "Just give me two more minutes."

"No problem," I told her, smiling at my reflection in the dressing room mirror. After all, I could spend another half-hour just daydreaming about the presents!

• • •

Okay, Ashley, I said to myself, *you saved the best dress for last. Time to go for it.*

I hung up all the outfits I'd already tried on. Then I turned and took the last dress down from the hook on the back of the door. I had a feeling that this was going to be *the one.*

I slipped the long, flowy, light-blue gown over my head, and it fell perfectly on my frame. The dress looked like it was made for me—it was just the right length, fit perfectly around the waist, and its slim spaghetti straps were totally flattering. Plus, it sparkled when the light hit it just right.

Mary-Kate is going to love this so much, I thought. *She's going to want to get the exact same dress!*

I gathered up my long, wavy blond hair into a twist and secured it with a clip. Then I stood up on my tiptoes and grinned at my reflection. I'd found it! The perfect outfit for our sweet sixteen . . .

Mary-Kate and I walk into a huge ballroom filled with people who are all dressed up in ball gowns and tuxedoes. Elegantly dressed waiters circle the room carrying trays heaped with food and tall champagne glasses full of sparkling cider. The scent of flowers fills the air, and there are roses on every table. Hundreds of candles give the room a romantic glow.

The dance floor gleams, and two incredibly cute

guys ask me and Mary-Kate to dance. Mom and Dad stand along the wall, watching us with proud smiles. One of the waiters wheels out a huge cake, and everyone sings to us. When we blow out the candles, the whole room bursts into applause.

It's the most amazing party anyone has ever attended.

I shook myself out of my daydream and smiled at my reflection once again. It was all coming together. *Our sixteenth birthday is less than two months away,* I thought, *and now I've found the perfect dress—an elegant dress that shows I'm not a kid anymore.*

"Ashley!" My sister groaned.

"Okay, I'm ready!" I stood and smoothed the dress once more. "Let's both come out on the count of three."

"Right," Mary-Kate said. "Here goes. One . . ."

"Two . . . ," I chimed in.

"Three!"

We both stepped out of our dressing rooms, took one look at each other and burst out laughing.

"Um . . . I think we may have a problem here," I said, taking in her shorts and tank top.

"Tell me about it, Cinderella," she joked. "Nice dress, though."

"Thanks, and those shorts are great. But . . ." I

shuffled over to her dressing room and peeked inside, taking in the piles of casual clothes. There wasn't a single dress in sight. "Mary-Kate, what were you thinking?"

"Beach party, of course!" she replied.

"But . . . we live in Malibu, California," I said. "We go to the beach all the time."

"Exactly," she said. "What's the point of living here if you don't take advantage of it?"

I took in her shorts and tank top again. When it came to our birthday party, we were definitely not on the same planet. "Maybe we should go somewhere and start talking about this party," I suggested.

Ashley and I kicked back in the cushy corner booth at Starbucks with our coffees. "We've got to get serious about this sweet sixteen party," she said. "I know you like to be spontaneous, but—"

"Hey," I protested. "Even I know that great parties take planning. Give me a *little* credit, Miss Organization."

She pulled out a glittery purple notebook and matching pen. "I'm no more organized than the average person," she insisted.

"Does the average person alphabetize all the books in her bedroom?" I asked. "Does the average person keep all of her drawers color coordinated? I don't think so."

"All right," she said, sniffing. "So I'm above average. I just can't live in total chaos—like *some* people I know."

"Hey," I protested. "I don't live in chaos. I just . . . go with the flow." Though I have to admit the floor of my room is littered with shoes and I'm always tripping over them.

"Whatever." She tapped her purple pen, ready to work. "Back to the party. Where do we start?"

I zipped up the front of my dark-blue hoodie and leaned my elbows on the table. "We've already been to a lot of sweet sixteens. Remember those goody bags from Sherra Cintron's party? With the CDs and the little disposable cameras? Those were cool."

"Yes! That *was* a good idea," Ashley agreed, making a note. "We could give out goody bags, too—something that goes along with our theme."

"Theme?" I flopped back against the velvety couch. "How are we supposed to find a theme that's got you wearing a ball gown and me hanging out in shorts and a T-shirt?"

"Okay, don't freak," Ashley said. "We'll just have to compromise, somehow."

"I know." I stirred my Frappuccino with my straw. "I just wish we weren't born so late in the year. It's like there's all this pressure to top the parties that came before ours."

Ashley smiled confidently. "Hey, this is *our* party," she said. "It'll blow all those other ones out of the water." She glanced down at her notebook. "Who should we invite?"

"I've been thinking a lot about this," I said, sitting up again. "I think it should be an all-girl party."

"Really?" Ashley asked.

"Yeah. None of our friends has a serious boyfriend," I pointed out. "And I think everyone would have a lot more fun if they weren't worried about looking cool in front of the guys."

Ashley frowned. "I see your point. But we *are* turning sixteen. Wouldn't it be kind of . . . I don't know . . . unsophisticated to have an all-girl party?"

"Having guys there won't make it sophisticated," I said. "Most of our guy friends still think burping contests rule."

Ashley giggled. Then a movement by the door caught her eye. "Hey, there's Lauren and Brittany!"

Sure enough, our two best friends were making their way over to our table. Lauren and Brittany couldn't be more different if they tried. Lauren is tall with wavy brown hair, light skin, and tons of freckles. She's always sweet to everyone and has an eternally sunny outlook. Brittany, on the other hand, can be sarcastic about anything—from breakfast cereal to biology class. She's African-American and has dark brown eyes and tight black

7

curls that she never lets grow past her earlobes.

Brittany waved to us. "Mary-Kate and Ashley—at Starbucks? What a shocker!"

"Hey, I'm not the one with the frequent-customer card," I shot back.

Lauren glanced down at Ashley's notebook.

"'Gift bags?'" she read. "For what?"

"We're trying to plan our sweet sixteen." Ashley sighed. "Unfortunately we haven't gotten very far."

"Ashley's thinking royal ball while I'm thinking beach party," I explained. "I picked out shorts and she picked out a dress . . . and she wants to invite the guys and I think it should be just girls."

Brittany laughed and shook her head, her dangly earrings jingling.

"Another shocker!" she joked. "Anyone who knows you two could have seen this coming."

"Are we that predictable?" Ashley asked.

"Kind of—in a good way," Lauren said. "But whatever you guys decide to do, I'm sure it'll be the best party ever. Everyone's already looking forward to it. I overheard Rachel and Alex talking about it the other day. They can't wait to see what you're going to do."

"No pressure or anything," Brittany cracked.

Pressure? I wasn't worried. A wave of calm washed over me.

Working together, Ashley and I would plan a

sweet sixteen to end all sweet sixteens—
I felt sure of it.

"Hey, we love pressure," I declared, leaning
back into the couch. "We *live* for pressure."

"Okay, let's talk about themes." Ashley flipped
her notebook to a new page. "What were some good
ones from parties we've gone to?"

Lauren's blue eyes brightened. "I loved the Paris
theme at Melanie Han's party, with the Eiffel Tower
replica and all the twinkling lights."

"Okay, so something international would be
good," Ashley said, making a note. "What else?"

"Hey! What about a Broadway theme?"
Brittany suggested. "Ashley loves acting, and you
could have a city skyline and playbills and stuff like
that."

"Good one!" Ashley said, writing it down.

"Or we could do a Hollywood thing," I added,
ideas starting to flit through my head. "We could
have a replica of the Hollywood sign, a red carpet—"

"Or what about a Hawaiian theme!" Ashley
chimed in. "Hula skirts, leis, coconuts, sand . . ."

"Or we could do a music theme—"

"Or Mardi Gras—"

"Guys!" Brittany cried, holding up her hands.
The rest of us stopped our babble fest. "Look who
just walked in," she whispered.

I looked up, and my breath caught in my throat.

Jake Impenna was headed for the coffee counter. Jake is an incredibly cute seventeen-year-old junior who just moved to Malibu a few months ago. His brown, spiky hair was hidden beneath a well-worn baseball cap, and he was wearing a gray T-shirt that matched his amazing eyes.

Jake was on the basketball and baseball teams at our school, Bayside High, and everyone saw him as this total jock. But he was also in my creative writing class, and I could tell from his stories that he had a seriously sensitive side. I had a monster crush on him, and my friends knew it. I felt their eyes on me while I stared at him.

"Are you gonna talk to him?" Brittany asked.

I blushed. "I don't feel like making an idiot of myself today."

Brittany raised her eyebrows. "Since when do you have trouble talking to anyone?"

"Since whenever Jake walks into a room," I answered. "I need at least half an hour to practice before I can even say hello to him."

"Well, start practicing," Ashley said.

My heart raced and my mouth went dry. Jake was weaving through the café with his coffee . . . and heading right for our table!

chapter two

"Hey, everybody," Jake said. He leaned his free hand on the back of an empty chair. "Mary-Kate," he added.

"Hi, Jake." My tongue felt dead inside my mouth, but I don't think Jake noticed.

"Did you finish that creative writing assignment yet?" he asked me.

"Not yet." I relaxed a little, glad that I didn't have to come up with something to talk about. "We have to write a poem about ourselves," I explained to my friends. "It's harder than it sounds."

"Seriously," Jake agreed. "I keep trying different things, but they all come out embarrassing. How about you?"

"Yeah . . . exactly." I gave a nervous little laugh. I didn't want to admit that every time I tried to write my poem, I thought of Jake. What if I had to read it out loud in class? What would he think of it?

11

The idea absolutely and totally paralyzed me.

An awkward silence fell over the group. My friends stared at me. I could tell what they were thinking. Their eyes practically screamed *Say something, stupid!*

I know! I wanted to shout back. *But I can't think of anything! Where are my jokes? Why can't I talk?*

"Whatever," Jake said. "You've probably never done anything embarrassing in your life."

"Uh . . . thanks." Was he kidding? Wasn't he witnessing my total lack of conversational skills?

"Well, good luck with the poem," Jake said. "I'll see you guys later."

He started to walk away, and Brittany widened her eyes at me. *Say something!* she mouthed.

"Like what?" I whispered back.

"Um, Jake?" Lauren piped up. "We were just wondering if . . . you're going to Todd Malone's beach party this weekend."

Nice save, Lauren! I thought.

Jake turned back to us. "I'm not sure I want to go. I'm getting a little beached out lately, you know?" He shrugged.

I sagged with disappointment. Todd's party would definitely be a lot less interesting without Jake.

"Oh, but you *should* come," Ashley insisted.

"Todd always throws the best parties."

"Yeah!" I broke in, finally finding my voice. "Ashley and I never miss them." *Great*, I thought. That *was impressive.*

Jake smiled slowly and looked directly at me. For a split second, it felt as if everyone else disappeared.

"In that case, I'll be there," he said.

My cheeks burned, but I managed to sound cool when I said, "See ya there!"

Jake lifted his coffee cup to say good-bye, then pushed his way through the door of the shop.

"Aaaaaa!" As soon as he was gone, we all squealed in excitement. I'm not normally a squealer, but I couldn't help myself.

"Did you hear that?" I cried.

"He *so* likes you," Brittany said.

"No!" I protested, waving her off, even though I was grinning so hard my face hurt.

"You know he does," Ashley put in. "He was practically drooling."

"And he *is* going to the party for you," Lauren said. "That was totally obvious."

I bit my lip as a little shiver went down my back. "It was, wasn't it?"

"Totally," Ashley confirmed. She took a sip of coffee, then pulled her notebook toward her. She loves to get things done. "Now, let's get back to our party. Where should we have it?"

Brittany and Lauren started to spout out different ideas for places to hold our sweet sixteen. I zoned out a little, thinking ahead to Todd's party. Suddenly I couldn't wait for the weekend!

"Mary-Kate, are you all right?" Mom asked me that night. "You've got the funniest expression on your face."

Ashley elbowed me. We were sitting down for dinner with our parents, and I knew what Mom was talking about—this ridiculous grin that just wouldn't go away. All I could think about was Jake. I kept playing his words over and over in my mind and coming to the same, undeniable conclusion. Jake definitely liked me! Or, at the very least, he wanted to see me at Todd's party, which was almost as good.

"I'm fine, Mom," I assured her. "I'm just in a good mood."

"I'm glad to hear that," Dad said as he sank into his seat at the head of the table. He pulled at his tie until it was loosened and then unbuttoned the top button of his shirt. "Because I have great news."

His blue eyes twinkled with excitement. It wasn't often that Dad came home from work looking this psyched. He's an executive at a big music company, and he always has to deal with people who have "big attitudes and even bigger egos" (or so he says), and it sometimes wears him down. He's been extra stressed lately because of this huge summer music festival he's been helping to plan. It was good to see him looking happy for a change.

"Don't keep them in suspense, honey." Mom laughed, tucking a few stray strands of her blond hair behind her ear.

"Well, I was meeting with this band called Rave today—"

"Wait a minute, *Rave*?" Ashley interrupted him, her eyes wide. "When did you guys sign Rave? They're one of my favorite bands! Dad, *please* tell me you're going to let us meet them."

I held my breath. Even though our father had access to all these incredibly cool people, Ashley and I had never met any of the musicians his label represented. He had a strict policy of keeping business separate from the family.

Of course, his policy didn't keep me and Ashley from begging every chance we got.

"No, honey," my father said slowly. Ashley's face fell. "But listen, girls, they had their party planner there with them. His name is Wilson Miller, and he's worked with a lot of our bands over the last couple of years. Great guy."

He paused to take a bite of his pasta. Ashley and I watched him chew, waiting to hear more. He chewed, and chewed, and chewed. . . .

"And?" I prompted when my father finally swallowed.

"And he owes me a favor, so when he heard you and Ashley had a sweet sixteen coming up, he offered to plan it for you," Dad announced. "Free of charge!"

"Isn't that great, girls?" Mom asked.

"I don't believe it!" Ashley exclaimed. "Rave's party planner working on *our* sweet sixteen?"

"That's incredible!" I flashed back to the fabulous pictures from swank celebrity parties I'd seen in fashion magazines. "This could be the biggest party of the year!"

"Thank you so much, Dad," Ashley said. "This is going to be so cool!"

"I'll set up a meeting for all of us." Dad smiled. "You girls are going to love Wilson."

I dug in to my food and realized my perma-grin had actually widened. But this time it wasn't because of Jake. Now I was imagining a Hollywood-worthy sweet sixteen!

Breathe, Ashley, I coached myself.

A few days later, Mary-Kate and I were in the backseat of Dad's car on our way to Wilson Miller's office. A bunch of nervous butterflies were holding a dance party in my stomach. After all, this guy had worked not only with Rave, but with a bunch of other bands at Dad's label. He'd hung with the coolest people on the planet! What if Mary-Kate and I didn't measure up?

Wilson worked out of his home—a huge, Spanish-style stucco ranch house that was built into the side of a hill. It was surrounded by palm trees and tropical flowers, and was totally secluded. I almost gasped when Dad pulled the car into the driveway. It was so beautiful! We made our way to the front door. I couldn't help imagining the star-studded parties Wilson had probably thrown there.

"Welcome to my abode!" Wilson said brightly when he opened the door.

I smiled the moment I saw him. Wilson was young and totally down with the latest trends. His hair was hidden under a burgundy-and-blue ski cap, and he was wearing a black T-shirt and seriously faded jeans. He was definitely cute, in a post-college-guy kind of way, and he had a cell phone in one hand and a pager in the other.

"Just give me one sec," he said as we stepped into the foyer. He held the cell phone to his ear while scrolling through messages on his pager. "Yeah . . . yeah, Carlos. I will definitely be in Grand Cayman tonight, but I have to leave for Aspen on Monday. Yeah . . . right. Looking forward to it. I have some people here, so I gotta go. Okay . . . later." He looked up at us and gave a casual shrug.

"So many plans, so little time. You know how it is."

Mom and Dad laughed, and Wilson turned to Mary-Kate and me. "So you're the infamous Mary-Kate and Ashley," he said, pretending to give us a once-over. "I've heard all about you from your father."

Mary-Kate groaned in mock horror. "I hope he didn't break out the baby pictures," she joked. "Because if he did, watch out. America's snooziest home videos are next."

Wilson laughed. I wished I could be more like Mary-Kate—she always knows just what to say to break the ice.

"Okay, we've got a lot to do, and I have got to get out of here in less than an hour." Wilson checked his watch. "So come on in."

We followed him into his office. Mary-Kate and I settled into the two soft chairs across from his desk. Mom and Dad took the couch in the back of the office, behind us.

"Okay." Wilson leaned his elbows on his desk. "The first thing I want to make clear is that I'm working for you. That means that my job is to do whatever you want me to do, and to do it right. I'm going to help you realize the party of your dreams."

I grinned at Mary-Kate, impressed. Talk about saying exactly what we wanted to hear!

"We're sold. Where do I sign?" Mary-Kate joked.

"Well, hold on." Wilson chuckled. "First let me show you some pictures from other parties I've thrown."

He opened a drawer and pulled out a thick, suede-covered photo album. I lifted myself up from my chair a bit so I could see the photos better.

I couldn't believe my eyes. I was looking at pictures from Jenna Rodenberry's wedding! There she was herself, cutting the cake! Jenna was one of the biggest movie stars in the world, and Wilson Miller had done her wedding!

"I can't believe it." I gasped.

I turned to Mary-Kate and saw her staring down at the page as if she couldn't tear her eyes away.

"Oh, but that's a wedding. You don't need to see that," Wilson said.

He turned to a page full of pictures taken at a dance club, all decked out for Halloween. The decorations were unreal. Every inch of wall was covered with cobwebs and fake spiders. Hanging from the ceiling were yards of black-and-orange crepe, and along the floor sat fat pumpkins carved so intricately they looked like sculptures.

"You are *seriously* detail-oriented," Mary-Kate said.

Wilson laughed. "That's my job. Let me show you an example of something more understated."

He flipped the page and smoothed the book

down in front of us. These pictures were from a much simpler party. It was a tropical theme with fresh flowers strewn all over the tables and colorful umbrellas ruffling in the breeze. Leis made of real flowers were draped over the backs of bamboo chairs. The waiters were wearing Hawaiian shirts with khaki shorts and sandals.

My skin tingled with excitement. Wilson Miller could be the secret weapon we needed to make our sweet sixteen the coolest one yet!

Mary-Kate raised her eyebrows, I nodded, and then we both looked at Wilson.

"Really, no joking . . . you're hired!" Mary-Kate announced.

"Great!" Wilson exclaimed. He looked over our heads at our parents. "That was easy!"

Mom and Dad laughed. "We're glad to have you on board," Mom said.

"So, let's get right down to it," Wilson said, closing the book and pulling it away. "What kind of party are you two thinking about throwing?"

I thought about the brainstorming session we'd had earlier in the week. I'd made about five pages of notes, but we had no clear idea of what we wanted.

I bit my lip. "Well, we haven't really decided on a theme yet," I said slowly.

"Let's just say, decision-making isn't our strong point," Mary-Kate added.

"That's all right," Wilson said. "A theme is a tough thing to settle on. It can make or break your whole party."

Tell me about it, I thought.

"I have a suggestion." Wilson stood up and walked over to a packed bookcase in the corner of the office.

He slipped out a thick album and brought it over to the desk. This one was filled with invitations.

He thumbed through the pages. "Take this home with you and try to pick out an invitation." He flipped through a huge array of different invites. "Sometimes the kind of invitation you choose can be a good jumping-off point for a theme."

"Great!" I said as he handed the book to me. I hugged it against my chest. "I can't wait to go through this."

"Yeah, thanks, Mr. Miller," Mary-Kate said, standing up. She offered her hand, and he shook it.

"Call me Wilson," he offered, letting go of Mary-Kate's hand and grasping my free one. "Call me as soon as you've decided, and we'll go from there. Your party date is only eight weeks from now—that's not as far away as it sounds. So let's try to settle some of the details this week. I'm never in one place for long, but you can always get me on my cell."

As Wilson walked our parents to the door, Mary-Kate and I practically ran to the car with the invitation book.

All I could think about was getting home and getting to work on the party. Soon Mary-Kate and I would have an invitation and a theme, and now that we had Wilson working with us, we were going to have the coolest sweet sixteen in history.

chapter three

"Another quiet Saturday night in Malibu," I joked as music blasted up to us from the beach.

I followed Ashley, Lauren, and Brittany around the side of Todd Malone's house toward the wooden staircase that led to the beach. We could see that the party below was already in full swing. There was a huge bonfire with tons of people crowded around it. Todd was barbecuing with some of the guys at an open grill. Dance music blasted from speakers placed around the fire, and a couple of dozen kids were dancing near the water.

"Now *this* is cool," I said.

"Todd's outdone himself this time," Lauren agreed as we picked our way carefully down the stairs.

Brittany flashed me her devilish grin. "So, do you think he's here yet?"

I felt a nervous twinge in the pit of my stomach.

23

"Who? Todd?" I asked, hoping to throw them off the subject of Jake Impenna. As if that were possible.

"No! Jake!" all three of them shouted in unison.

I stopped in the middle of the staircase. "Say it a little louder!" I told them. "I think there are a few fish out there who didn't hear you."

"Sorry." Ashley bit her lip. "No more Jake talk. We promise."

"Thank you!" I said as we continued down the steps.

Of course, as soon as we were close enough to see everyone, I found myself scanning the faces of the party goers, looking for Jake. It took me about five seconds to spot him standing with a few guys over by the food.

He looked up and caught my eye. Then he smiled, and I instantly blushed. I was glad that I was so close to the bonfire. I could pretend I was just flushed from the heat.

"Hey, there's Tashema and Melanie." Brittany grabbed my hand and started to pull me toward the water. "Let's dance!"

"Okay! I'm coming!" I laughed, grabbing Ashley and Lauren as well. Brittany could not control herself if there was a dance floor nearby.

The music mixed with the sound of crashing waves and made it a pretty loud scene. We shouted our hellos to Melanie and Tashema and started dancing.

"This is a great setup!" I said to Ashley, leaning in close to her ear so I could be heard. "It's kind of like what I was thinking about for our sweet sixteen."

"I can see that." Ashley frowned as she looked around. "Maybe we should compromise and—"

I grabbed Ashley's wrist and froze. She stopped midsentence. She followed my gaze and saw what—-I mean, *who*—had paralyzed me.

Jake Impenna was cutting across the dance floor and honing in on us. I had no idea what to do. What should I say to him? Should I act happy to see him? Should I be aloof? Should I panic and run away?

Ashley gave me a little shake. "Snap out of it!" she whispered. "Dance!" She started dancing again. I tried to dance, but my feet felt like lead.

"Hey!" Jake called as he slid past a couple of people to dance with Ashley and me. "I'm glad you showed!"

"Yeah! Me, too," I said. "I mean . . . you, too." Oh, no! I was making no sense again! Why did Jake have such a weird effect on me?

Maybe because he's older, and gorgeous and athletic and smart and . . . perfect! I thought.

"I mean, I'm glad you showed, too," I added, finally getting my point across.

"Thanks." Jake laughed.

We all danced together, and, after a few minutes,

I relaxed a bit. Then, when Jake had his back turned, Ashley tapped my arm and whispered, "I'll be right back."

My breath caught, and I tried to grab her hand, but she just waved and disappeared. My pulse pounded like crazy. How could my sister leave me on the dance floor with Jake? What if he thought I wanted to dance alone with him but he didn't want to dance alone with me?

I was going to have to kill her.

Then, out of nowhere, the hip-hop song that was playing cut off and one of my favorite slow songs came on. Everyone paused for a moment, but soon the crowd started to pair off, and couples dotted the dance floor, swaying slowly to the music.

Jake raised his eyebrows. "Wanna dance?"

My heart melted. He was too cute for words!

"Sure." I reached up and wrapped my arms around his neck as he put his around my waist.

Before I knew it, we were moving together to the perfect, romantic slow song. Me and Jake Impenna! Slow dancing! I couldn't believe it. Over his shoulder, I spotted Ashley standing by the stereo. She waved, and I realized what she'd done. Oh, my gosh. She'd changed the song just so that I could dance with Jake! Suddenly, I didn't feel so much like strangling her anymore.

Ashley flashed me a thumbs-up sign. I shook

my head. What would I do without her?

When the song came to an end, I reluctantly pulled away from Jake. People began to walk away from the dance floor, heading for the barbecue. I hesitated for a second. I didn't want this part of the night to end.

"So . . . ," Jake said.

"So. . . ." I laughed nervously. *Say something!* I told myself, but my brain refused to cooperate.

"Listen, I know this is kind of out of nowhere, but do you think . . . I mean, would you like to go out with me sometime?" he asked.

I forced myself to look into his gray eyes. I had to make sure he wasn't joking. No, I realized. He meant it.

I felt like blurting out "Yes!" at the top of my lungs. *Stay cool, stay cool*, I warned myself. I took a deep breath and smiled up at him.

"Sure," I said. "That sounds great."

A huge smile lit his face.

"Excellent," he said. "How's Friday? I was thinking dinner and a movie or something like that. Can I pick you up around six?"

"That would be perfect," I replied.

"Perfect," Jake repeated. "Then I guess I'll . . . talk to you later." He turned and started up the beach, following the rest of the crowd.

"Yeah! Later!" I said, lifting my hand. I didn't

even know what I was doing or saying. All I knew was that Jake Impenna had actually asked me out!

When he was a safe distance away, I scanned the crowd for my sister and spotted her hanging with a couple of people by the fire. I half ran, half skipped over to her. I could barely contain my excitement.

"What happened?" Ashley said.

"He asked me out!" I whispered, grasping her arms. "We're going out on Friday!"

Ashley let out a squeal and hugged me. "I knew it!" she cried. "I knew he was going to!"

"Thank you so much!" I said when we pulled away from each other. "You totally set the mood with that slow song."

Ashley grinned. I could tell she was happy for me. "Hey, that's what sisters are for."

A little while later, Mary-Kate and I were getting ourselves a couple of sodas. Mary-Kate was still completely giddy over Jake.

"You don't understand," she said, all starry-eyed. "He's not just a super-jock. You should hear the stuff he writes for class. He can be totally mushy."

"He sounds really sweet," I told her, taking a sip of my soda. "I'm so psyched for you!"

"I know! Me, too," Mary-Kate said. "So where's

Brittany?" she asked, looking around. "I haven't seen her since he asked me out and I already told Lauren, Tashema, and Melanie. If Brittany hears this from someone else, I'm a dead girl."

"She's over there, shamelessly flirting with Michael Gelb." I pointed her out to Mary-Kate. Brittany stood by the stereo, sorting through CDs with Michael and giggling like crazy. "You tell her. I'm going to go get some food."

"I'll be right back." Mary-Kate took off down the beach.

I spun around to head for the barbecue and smacked right into someone. I managed to stay on my feet, but the poor, unsuspecting guy was sent sprawling onto the sand. A bunch of people standing around us laughed.

"I am so sorry!" I cried. My victim sat up and dusted the sand from the front of his black concert T-shirt.

"Hey, no problem," he responded, smiling up at me. "It's not a party until someone lands on their butt."

I didn't mean to stare at him, but I couldn't help it. This guy was cute. Incredibly cute. His shaggy brown hair fell into his eyes—the warmest brown eyes I had ever seen. I reached out to help him up. When he grabbed my hand, my heart gave a little extra thump.

29

"Are you okay?" I asked, letting go of his hand.

"No harm done," he said, waving me off. "But I am going to warn my friends to keep a safe distance from you," he joked.

I just kept staring at him. His smile . . . it was kind of mischievous. Kind of sly.

What's wrong with me? I thought. *Say something, Ashley! Something funny like Mary-Kate would.* But I couldn't. I was totally speechless.

"Uh . . . right," I mumbled. "Good idea."

"I'm just kidding." The guy stared at me like I was insane.

"No! I know. Of course you were. I just . . . I *am* a klutz so it would probably be a good idea for you to . . . you know . . ."

Stop talking, Ashley! Just stop talking!

"Warn my friends?" he supplied, putting me out of my misery.

"Yeah," I said with a laugh.

"Okay. Well, I'll see ya." He jogged off and joined a group of people who were down by the DJ, getting the dancing going again. I opened my mouth to call after him. I wanted to ask him his name, but he was too far away.

Instead, I searched the crowd and found Lauren at a table over by the barbecue, chowing down on cheeseburgers with Melanie and Tashema.

"What's up?" Lauren asked.

"Not much," I told her, glancing at the dance floor. Mystery Boy was hamming it up with a few of his friends.

"Do any of you know who that guy is?" I asked, tilting my head in Mystery Boy's direction. "The one in the black T-shirt and the green cargo pants?"

Tashema slowly shook her head, her beaded braids clicking together. "No clue," she said. "Why? Are you thinking that both twins are going to get lucky in love tonight?"

"Yeah, right," I scoffed.

"I've never seen him before," Melanie added, putting her fork down and wiping her fingers on a napkin. "But he is seriously cute—if you go for the just-this-side-of-grungy type. Maybe he's from Harrison High."

"Yeah! Todd does know a lot of people from Harrison, remember?" Tashema said. "He lived over there until seventh grade, and he stayed friends with a lot of those guys."

Harrison High. It wasn't a lot to go on, but it was definitely a place to start.

I pulled out the plastic chair next to Lauren's and sat down, watching Mystery Boy, who was still dancing. Who did Todd know from Harrison High? I had to admit I had absolutely no idea.

But when I pictured Mystery Boy's lopsided grin, I knew that somehow, I had to find out.

31

I never felt so attracted to anyone so fast! That had to mean something, I thought. And after all, maybe Tashema was right. Now that Mary-Kate had a date with a really cute guy, I was starting to think I should have one, too!

chapter four

I crossed my legs Indian style on Mary-Kate's bed as she sat down next to me. "Okay, so . . . what do we want our invitation to say?" I asked, opening Wilson's big book of invitations next to my party-planning notebook.

It was late on Friday afternoon. We'd decided to figure out the whole invitation issue before Jake picked Mary-Kate up for their date.

"The usual," Mary-Kate said absently. She stared off into space, fiddling with her rings. "Date, time, place . . ."

I laughed as I picked up one of Mary-Kate's gray flannel throw pillows—and whacked her over the head with it.

"Hey!" She scowled at me. "What was that for?"

"I know what we want it to *say*, I mean what kind of message should it send?" I clarified. "You know, is this a *cool* party, a *casual* party, a *dressy* party. . . . What planet are you on, anyway?"

"Planet Jake," Mary-Kate admitted, shaking her head at herself. "Sorry. I'm going to focus now, I promise."

"That's okay. I totally understand," I said. "Let's just get this done. Then we can concentrate on picking out something for you to wear on your date."

"Deal," Mary-Kate agreed.

We paged through the book past invitations that were too frilly, too plain, or too cute. None of them were quite right. Finally, Mary-Kate turned the page, and we both paused.

"Ooooh," I said. *This* I like."

Right smack in the middle of the page was the perfect invitation. It was a real CD with a sample photo of a girl and the details of her party printed on it. It was made to look as if the girl was a pop star and recorded the CD herself. A note beside the disk said that it was a real CD—you could burn any song or message you wanted on it. The lettering and design were totally funky and said exactly what I thought our invitation should say. *"This party is going to be fun and completely hip."*

"I love it!" Mary-Kate said. "Even the envelope is cool!"

The envelope was a cardboard CD sleeve—just like the ones record companies used when they were promoting a new band.

"I think we found our invitation," I said.

"Definitely," Mary-Kate said. "*And* you get to scratch something off your to-do list!" she added, teasing me.

"Ha, ha," I said flatly, even though she was right. I loved getting things done! I pulled my purple notebook over and carefully copied down the item number from the invitation book. "Everyone is going to love these!"

"One problem," Mary-Kate said, squirming her way up into a seated position. "Wilson said our invitation would be a . . . what did he call it again?"

I frowned and looked down at the invitation. "A jumping-off point."

"Yeah," Mary-Kate said. "And this would be good for any kind of party. I mean, we'll have music no matter what."

I sighed, realizing Mary-Kate was right. It was a great invitation, but it didn't get us much closer to deciding on the theme.

"Oh, well." I shrugged. "We'll just have to figure out the theme another time, I guess."

I reached over the side of her bed, grabbed my backpack, and pulled out my planner. Wilson had called with a few deadlines the other day, and I'd written them all down in my date book.

"We're doing fine," I told Mary-Kate. "We've got six weeks until the party. We'll call Wilson tomorrow with the item number so he can order the invitations, and that'll be done on time. We'll get him the theme next week, and he doesn't need the guest list until a few days after that."

I scanned the calendar to see if there was anything else we had to do and noticed a big star on Monday.

"Driver's Ed starts next week," I reminded Mary-Kate. "Our first step toward total freedom!"

"I can't wait to see you behind the wheel," Mary-Kate joked. "People of Malibu, run for your lives!"

"Hey!" I protested. "I may be a klutz on my feet, but I know I'll be a great driver."

"It'll be so cool," Mary-Kate said. "We'll be able to go wherever we want, whenever we want."

I flopped back on the bed, staring up at the ceiling. I pictured the two of us cruising the coast in Dad's SUV. (It was a totally parental car, but at least it was better than Mom's Volvo.)

I twisted a few strands of hair around my finger. "We'll go to the beach by ourselves, go to the mall without Mom looking over our shoulder. Where do you think we should drive ourselves first?"

There was no answer.

"Mary-Kate?" I prompted.

Nothing.

I sat up and looked at her. "Mary-Kate?"

"What?" she asked, snapping out of a blank-faced stare. The girl had obviously been off on Planet Jake again.

I hit her with the pillow one more time for good measure, then pushed myself off her bed. "I think it's time to start picking out your clothes for tonight."

"How do I look?" I asked, stepping in front of the full-length mirror that hung on the back of my door.

Ashley and I were standing in the middle of my bedroom with clothes scattered everywhere—on the floor, the bed, my desk chair, the dresser. . . . Some of the stuff was mine, some of it was Ashley's. We'd even swiped a couple of sweaters from Mom's closet.

"You look amazing." Ashley stepped up to admire me in the mirror. I was wearing my favorite lavender halter top with Ashley's favorite slim black pants. How could I go wrong?

I turned to check myself out from the side. "Not too overdressed, right?" I asked.

"No. It's perfect for dinner and a movie," Ashley said.

A nervous chill crept down my back. In a few minutes Jake and I would be out alone together! "What if we don't have anything to talk about?" I asked, my pulse starting to pound. "I don't even know if we have anything in common."

"Of course you do!" Ashley said. "You go to the same school, you know all the same people, you both take creative writing—"

"Yeah, but how long can two people talk about a class?" I asked, swallowing hard.

"Mary-Kate, it's going to be fine. It shouldn't be too hard to make dinner conversation. Especially for you."

"Right." I sat down on my bed and breathed deeply to calm my nerves. "But I really like him, Ashley. I want everything to be perfect. And you saw me go wordless when he talked to us at Starbucks the other day."

"Mary-Kate, you have nothing to worry about," Ashley promised. She sat down next to me and put an arm around my shoulders. She gave me a little squeeze. "Jake already likes you. If he didn't, he wouldn't have asked you out."

"True," I said slowly, staring down at a pile of clothes on the floor.

"All you have to do is be yourself," Ashley assured me.

"Okay, be myself," I said. I took another deep breath. "It's going to be fine. My first real date with an older, totally gorgeous guy is going to be perfect, fun, and totally mistake free." For a split second, I felt better. Then I remembered what I was *really* nervous about.

"Ashley?" I said. "What if he tries to kiss me?"

"Then you'll kiss him back." Ashley shrugged.

"Come on!" I stood and started to pace. "Jake's older. He's probably gone on lots of dates. Kissed tons of girls! What if he wants to kiss me like . . . I mean . . . a *real* kiss?"

Ashley grabbed my shoulders and looked me right in the eye. "Mary-Kate! Chill!" she said firmly. She pulled me over to the mirror again, and we both got in real close, standing next to one another.

"Now, if he goes in for the kiss, this is what you do," Ashley said, shaking her hair behind her shoulders. "First, you tilt your head just a little like this." She tilted her head just to the right, so I imitated her.

"We look ridiculous," I said.

"Shhh!" she said. "Now, pucker your lips a little. Like this." Ashley demonstrated, pursing her lips. I did the same, but then I cracked up laughing.

"Come on!" Ashley said, grabbing my hand and pursing her lips again. "This is important."

"Okay! Okay!" I stifled my laughter. I took a deep breath and mimicked her.

"Mary-Kate! Jake is here!" Mom called up the stairs.

"I'll be right down!" I shouted back, happy to

hear that my voice didn't crack from nervousness.

"Just be yourself and have fun," Ashley advised me.

I nodded and smiled, but then I realized I was holding my breath. My nerves were totally fried, and "be yourself" seemed like pretty basic advice. Could it really be that easy?

"Thanks, Ashley," I said.

I grabbed my bag, tossed my hair back, and strode out of my room, making sure to hold my head up high. Easy or not, I was about to find out.

chapter five

I sprawled out in the big cushy chair in our living room with a bowl of popcorn on my lap. "I wonder how Mary-Kate is doing on her date," I muttered. "What time is it?"

"It's eight-oh-four," Brittany replied. "Exactly one minute after the last time you asked. Now pay attention to the movie, Ashley—this is the best part!"

Brittany and Lauren had come over, and we were watching *Always a Bridesmaid*, one of my all-time favorite movies. It had everything—cute guy, beautiful girl, romance, and lots of wedding dresses.

I was having a hard time concentrating, though. I couldn't stop thinking about Mary-Kate's date with Jake. They were probably finishing up dinner . . . unless they had to wait for a table. Where did Jake take her for dinner? What did she order? She was so nervous before she left! I really hoped it all went well. No, not just well. I wanted it to be absolutely perfect!

I glanced at the movie. It was the scene where the bridesmaid accidentally messes up her friend's wedding. "This is Mary-Kate's favorite part," I noted. "She knows these lines by heart." I felt a quick pang in my chest. "You know, I wish she were here with us. I miss her."

Brittany snorted. "You miss Mary-Kate? You guys must spend twenty hours a day together. She's only been gone for two hours."

I laughed. "I know. It's silly."

"I think it's sweet," Lauren put in. "I wish I was as close to my sister as you and Mary-Kate are."

When the movie ended a little while later, Lauren clicked the TV off and leaned back in her seat. "I love that movie," she said wistfully. "The wedding at the end is so beautiful. It's like the party of my dreams!"

Brittany pushed herself up in her seat and brushed a few popcorn crumbs from the front of her sweater. "Speaking of parties, what's up with your sweet sixteen? Have you and Mary-Kate been able to agree on anything yet?"

"Well, we picked out an invitation tonight," I told her. I set the popcorn bowl on the table. "We didn't have any trouble agreeing on that. Want to see it?"

Lauren's eyes brightened. "Totally!"

"I'll be right back." I jumped from my seat and jogged upstairs to my room to grab the invitation book. I ran back downstairs again, and Brittany and Lauren both scooted over, making room for me on the couch.

"I love it!" Lauren exclaimed when she saw the CD.

"We've already picked out the photo we're going to use," I said. "And the party planner is going to have Rave record a message for us! When you play the CD, it'll be like Rave is inviting you to our party!"

"Rave?" Lauren asked. "You mean the real Rave? The girl group?"

I nodded. "Wilson's pretty close with them. He said he could get them to do it, no problem."

"Wow! That is totally amazing!" Brittany said. "Even the guys will like it—if you're inviting guys. Are you inviting guys?"

I shrugged. "We haven't decided yet, but Mary-Kate seemed pretty set on an all-girl party. The more I think about it, the more I think it might be okay. It could be fun."

"Definitely." Lauren nodded. "Who needs guys to have a good time?"

"Speak for yourself," Brittany protested. Then she broke into a grin. "Just kidding. We all know that guys have their uses, but girls rule!"

My thoughts turned back to Mary-Kate. I hoped she was at least having a good time with the guy she was with tonight! I checked my watch again, wondering what time their movie started. I couldn't wait for her to get home so I could hear all about her date!

"Great choice, Jake! I've been dying to try this place, ever since it opened," I gushed.

The two of us were settled at a cozy table at Giovanelli's, the newest, most romantic Italian restaurant in town. I hadn't stopped smiling since Jake pulled into the parking lot. It was as if he knew exactly where I'd want to go.

I'd often dreamed of going on a date to a romantic restaurant just like this. But now that I was there, my nerves were on edge. There were so many potential disasters just waiting to happen! I could knock over a water glass or burn myself on the candle. I snatched a breadstick and bit it. It deteriorated into powder, spraying crumbs on the tablecloth and all over my lap.

After that, I was afraid to touch anything. I sat still with my hands clenched together in my lap.

"Now that you're here, what do you think of it?" Jake asked me. "Because if you don't like it we can go somewhere else."

He raised his eyes from his menu. He looked

cuter than ever in the candlelight. He was wearing a blue shirt and chinos, and he'd done something different to his hair. Gel or something. Did he realize how great he was? And did he know that he could date almost any girl at Bayside High?

"No—it's great!" I lifted my hand to wave off the suggestion—and knocked my spoon clear off the table. It landed somewhere across the room with a loud clatter. "I mean, I love this place," I said, trying to act as if nothing had happened. Inside, however, I was shrinking to the size of a peanut from embarrassment.

Jake glanced in the direction of my projectile spoon, then smiled.

"Good," he said. "It was either this or the Burger Shack, so . . ."

"Good choice," I said with a little laugh.

He sipped his water and examined his menu. I watched him, amazed at how cool and collected he seemed. Why wasn't he as freaked out and nervous as I was?

Calm down, I told myself. I picked up my menu and tried to study the different dishes, all of which were written in Italian. *If the spoon thing is the worst that happens tonight, you'll be fine.*

"Are you ready to order?" the waiter said, coming up to the table with his pen and pad ready.

"Mary-Kate?" Jake prompted politely.

I'd barely had time to read the menu. Flushed and confused, I scanned it quickly and ordered the first thing I recognized.

"Spaghetti?" I blurted, looking up at the waiter.

"Of course, miss," the waiter said. "Would you like that with bolognese, marinara, or primavera?"

"Uh, primavera," I answered.

I lifted the menu to hand it to the waiter. It clipped the side of my water glass and the glass tipped over! Water splashed across the tablecloth and all over the waiter's apron, shirt, and right in his face!

"I'm so sorry!" I gasped. I wished the earth would open up beneath me and swallow me whole.

Jake pulled his napkin from his lap and handed it to the stunned waiter, who thanked him and used it to wipe his face.

"It's no problem, miss," the waiter said kindly. "Happens all the time."

I laughed nervously, but I knew he was just trying to make me feel better. This couldn't happen all the time! If people were always messing up like this on first dates, there would be no couples in the world!

Jake placed his order, then looked across the table at me. "You okay?" he asked.

"Yes," I said. "You'd better watch out, though. Who knows what I'll do next?"

"Thanks for the warning," Jake teased. "So, how's the whole poem thing going?"

"Don't even ask." I rolled my eyes. "I haven't had much time to work on it. How about you?"

"I'm just hoping Ms. Trauth doesn't make us read them in front of the class," he said. "I hate that."

"Really?" I asked, surprised. "You'd never know it. You always look totally comfortable up there."

"Are you kidding?" Jake shook his head. "I'd rather have to make a million game-saving penalty shots than get up there and read for five seconds."

I smiled, amazed. Here I thought Jake was this totally together, popular jock who always knew the right thing to do, but it turned out he got nervous just like everyone else.

I sat back in my chair, waiting for him to say something else, but a silence fell over the table and stayed there for way too long. I realized with a start that it was actually my turn to speak.

Just think of something, I thought. *Anything!* I glanced at Jake, who was obviously as freaked as I was by the lack of conversation. He looked away, took another sip of his water, and cleared his throat.

My hands were actually shaking. Why was this happening to me? I could make conversation with anyone from the little old lady who worked at the grocery store to the five-year-olds at Mom's daycare center. And I'd always been fine on dates I'd had in the past. Why was I at a total loss now when it was so important?

Maybe it's because *it's so important,* I realized.

"Here you go!" the waiter said, arriving with our meals and finally breaking the silence.

He placed a huge bowl of spaghetti in front of me. It was still steaming from the kitchen, and it smelled incredible. Then he served Jake his chicken-and-pasta dish. I took a deep breath and picked up my fork as the waiter added a basket of freshly baked bread to the center of the table and refilled my water glass. I was so glad the food had arrived. At least we had something to concentrate on besides the silence!

"This looks great," Jake said, digging in. He cut a piece of his chicken and took a bite, smiling the moment he tasted it.

"Good?" I asked, twirling my fork around in my spaghetti.

"Awesome," Jake answered after he swallowed. "How's yours?"

"I'm about to find out," I said, picking up my fork.

Yikes! All but one strand of the spaghetti slipped right off and fell back to the plate. *Stay calm,* I told myself. I tried once more, twirling the fork in one of the thickest parts of the hill of pasta.

The fork was loaded, with long strands of spaghetti still dangling onto the plate. I sighed. *There's no good way for me to eat this*, I realized. *It's going to be a mess!*

I glanced at Jake, and he was watching me, waiting to see what I thought of my dinner. I plastered a brave smile on my face. Then I brought the fork to my mouth and hoped for the best.

I took as big a bite as I could, but three or four long pieces of spaghetti hung awkwardly from my lips. I quickly slurped them down. It was *definitely* not ladylike.

"How is it?" Jake asked.

"Great!" I murmured, nodding, my mouth still full. And it was. Unfortunately I wasn't going to be able to eat any more of it. I couldn't spend the whole dinner slurping and wiping, slurping and wiping. Ugh! Jake would be disgusted!

"I thought we could try to catch the eight-thirty show of *Off the Hook*," Jake suggested. "What do you think?"

I glanced at Jake to see if he was joking, but his beautiful gray eyes were entirely serious. I couldn't believe it. *Off the Hook* was supposed to be the stupidest movie of all time.

"*Off the Hook*, huh?" I repeated, stalling.

"Yeah! I've been waiting for it to come out forever," Jake said. "I love the director."

The director! I thought, a little shocked. *The same guy who did* Pigs in a Blanket? *The worst movie I've ever seen?*

Be open-minded, I decided. *Who knows? Maybe the movie won't be so bad.* "Ummm . . . I guess it could be funny," I said with a shrug.

"Great!" Jake said. "Maybe we should skip dessert here and just go crazy at the snack bar."

"Now you're talking." I started to relax a little. "I'd rather have a tub of popcorn and some gummy bears than a piece of cheesecake any day."

Jake grinned. "Gummi Bears and popcorn, huh? That's exactly what I get whenever I go to the movies."

"Really?" I said. We had the exact same taste in junk food! I knew I liked this guy for a reason.

I buttered a piece of bread, feeling a bit more comfortable. Maybe this date was going to shape up after all. Of course, I couldn't help glaring down at my spaghetti.

I made a mental note: Never order pasta on a date!

I sat in the dark theater next to Jake, munching hungrily on Gummi Bears. As predicted, the movie was truly horrible.

Jake laughed at the film, then shifted in his seat. His arm brushed mine, sending a little shiver of excitement over my skin. *He's so good-looking,* I thought. *He even smells good!* He glanced over at me, and I smiled.

You can do this, I told myself. *You can sit through this movie. It's for a very good cause . . . Jake Impenna!*

I started to slouch, so I moved back in my seat, trying to sit up straight. My Gummi Bear box hit the armrest and slipped from my hand. I held my breath as it clattered to the floor. The guy in front of us turned around and glared at me.

"Sorry!" I whispered.

I bent down to retrieve the box, but at that moment, Jake did the same, and we knocked heads—hard.

"Ow!" Jake moaned, bringing his hand to his forehead. "Sorry," he whispered.

"It's okay," I whispered back, my head throbbing.

Jake stared into my eyes, and I froze. He looked really serious all of a sudden. Was he going to try to kiss me now?

"Let's leave," Jake whispered.

My jaw dropped open. He wanted to leave? Was he having that bad of a time?

Of course he is, I thought. *All night I've been nothing but klutzy, messy, and dull. Why wouldn't he want to cut the night short?*

I was totally mortified, but there was nothing I could do. I wasn't going to *make* him sit there.

"Oh . . . okay," I said quietly.

Jake stood and led the way out of our nearly deserted row. It was all I could do to keep from bursting into tears behind his back. I wanted to go out with Jake Impenna from the first time I saw him. Now that I finally got my chance, what did I do? I totally blew it.

chapter six

"Mary-Kate, did you have a bad time tonight?" Jake asked. He had just pulled his Jeep up in front of my house. He sounded as tense as I felt.

"No!" I blurted kind of loudly. The word hung in the air for a second and then I laughed uncertainly. "I mean, I was kind of nervous and everything, and, to be honest, I wasn't really into the movie . . . but I liked . . . being with you."

Oh, smooth, Mary-Kate, I thought.

"I liked being with you, too," Jake said.

"Well . . . good." I laughed. "Glad we cleared that up."

Jake glanced at me out of the corner of his eye. "I feel like an idiot for picking that movie. It was so bad!"

"Wait a minute." I was confused. "I thought you liked it!"

He shook his head. "I was faking it. I just

laughed when the other people in the theater did because I didn't want you to think *I* was having a bad time."

I smiled, relieved. "And I just sat there with a smile plastered on my face so *you'd* think *I* was having a good time."

For a moment, neither of us said anything. Then Jake spoke up. "Hey, I'd like to hang out with you again. How about after school sometime?"

A second date! I thought. *He wants a second date!*

"How about Monday?" I blurted out.

Jake frowned. "Actually, that's not good for me. I take my little brother and sister to the park on Mondays. It's really important to them—we do it every week, so I can't cancel."

"Well, I love kids. Why don't I just come along with you?" I asked.

Jake frowned. "Are you sure? It wouldn't be anything big—"

"Absolutely! It sounds like total fun!" I insisted.

Jake grinned. "You know, I think Caitlin and Tristan would really like that."

Amazing. Jake wasn't just cute. He was so sweet that he made time to play with his little brother and sister!

"I'll be there," I told him.

"Great," Jake said. "We'll leave right from school, if that's cool with you."

"Definitely." I unbuckled my seat belt. "So . . . thank you so much for tonight. Dinner and half a movie."

"No problem." Jake started to climb out of the car. "Let me walk you to the door."

The second he started to move, I realized that the whole kiss question was back on. Nervous butterflies flittered through my stomach.

As we walked toward my front door, I landed on my high heel wrong and stumbled. Jake had to reach out to steady me.

"You okay?" he asked, gripping my arms.

"Yeah . . . fine." I pulled away slightly and stood up straight.

I glanced up at the house and spotted Ashley at the window, peeking through the curtain. I quickly waved her away. The curtain dropped, and Ashley's face disappeared just before Jake could see what I was looking at.

"You really don't have to walk me up," I said. "I've done it on my own a million times."

Jake chuckled. "Okay," he said. "Then I guess, if you don't mind, I'll kiss you good-night right here."

The direct approach! I liked it! He leaned in to kiss me. My heart pounded so quickly I was sure I was going to pass out right there.

This was it! Our first kiss!

Just as his lips met mine, something moved in

the window. I turned my head and saw Ashley's grinning face again. Jake's kiss landed on my earlobe.

"Whoa! Uh, sorry," I muttered nervously as he pulled away.

I turned my eyes toward him. He was blushing as hard as I was! We both cracked up laughing.

"I'll see you Monday," I said through my giggles.

"Right . . . Monday." Jake nodded.

I turned and started up the path to the house, but stopped midway and turned around.

"Thanks again, Jake. Tonight really was . . . interesting."

"Yeah. It sure was." I could tell by his grin that he meant, *interesting in a good way*.

I turned around and jogged into the house.

The moment Mary-Kate came through the front door, I grabbed her arm and pulled her into the living room. I was ready to burst. "So? How was it? Did he take you to a good restaurant? What movie did you see? Details! I need details!"

I couldn't wait a second longer to hear all about my sister's first date with the guy of her dreams.

We flopped down on the couch. Her eyes were shining brightly. I knew everything had gone perfectly. Why else would she be walking on air?

"Well, let's see, we went to Giovanelli's and I got

spaghetti, which was a mistake," Mary-Kate began. "Every time I slurped up a piece, the sauce splattered everywhere. Oh! But that was after I dumped my water on the waiter and flung my spoon across the room."

"You what?"

"Not on *purpose*," Mary-Kate assured me. As if that explained everything. "Then we went to see the worst movie ever—*Off the Hook*. So bad. I dropped my candy, we knocked heads, left early, came back here, and when he tried to kiss me I turned my head and he ended up kissing my ear."

I stared at my sister. She sighed and leaned into the back of the couch, gazing off into the distance as if she was replaying a wonderful romantic memory in her mind.

"Um . . . Mary-Kate?" I started.

She snapped out of her daydream and looked at me. "Yeah?"

"What are you so happy about? Everything on your date went wrong," I told her.

"That's just it!" she exclaimed, whacking my leg to make a point. "Everything went wrong and we still had a great time! There were one or two awkward silences, but the rest of the night, we totally connected. He even asked me out again!"

It was great to see her so happy. "Well then . . . I'm glad you had such a bad date!" I exclaimed.

"Jake sounds like he's a really great guy."

"I know!" Mary-Kate agreed. "I can't wait to see him again." She leaned over to the coffee table and grabbed one of the nearly empty bowls of popcorn. "Did you have fun with Brittany and Lauren?"

"Yeah, we watched *Always a Bridesmaid* and gorged ourselves on junk food. You know, the usual." I shrugged. "Oh, and I showed them the invitation. They loved it!"

"Good!" Mary-Kate said. "I can't wait to send them out." She twisted in her seat and put her feet up on the table, crossing them at the ankles.

"Lauren and Brittany are jealous that we're going to be getting our driver's licenses before them," I told her. "I promised them we'd drive them everywhere until their birthdays. I can't believe we're starting Driver's Ed on Monday."

"Oh, no!" Mary-Kate slapped her forehead. "I totally forgot about Driver's Ed. I told Jake I'd go to the park with him on Monday."

"So? Just call him and tell him you'll do it another time," I suggested.

"I can't!" Mary-Kate said, dropping her feet to the floor with a thud. "I made a really big deal about going to the park with him and his little brother and sister! After all the craziness on our date tonight, I don't want to call him and cancel our second date! He'll think I'm nuts."

"So what are you going to do?" I asked her, baffled. "Not take Driver's Ed?"

Mary-Kate munched on her popcorn, mulling it over. "Wait a minute!" she cried. "Isn't there a Tuesday/Thursday class? Let's switch to that one!"

"I can't," I said. "I have drama club on Tuesday afternoons. That's why we signed up for Monday/Wednesday in the first place, remember?"

Mary-Kate squeezed her eyes shut and groaned. "Right," she said. "Well, then I guess I'll switch by myself. It's no big deal, right? We'll just take Driver's Ed on different days."

She grabbed some more popcorn. I sat beside her, stunned. We always did *everything* together, and now that we were about to take what was basically the most important step of our lives, she wanted to split up?

"Ashley?" Mary-Kate eyed me. "That's okay, right?"

No, it's not okay! I wanted to shout. But I couldn't. Mary-Kate was so happy about Jake, I couldn't make a big deal about this. I didn't want to bring her down.

"Sure!" I said with a hollow smile, forcing myself to sound cheerful.

"Cool." She flicked on the television. "When you get home on Monday you can tell me all about it so I'll know what to expect."

"Yeah. That'll be . . . great," I said.

I leaned back into the couch and slouched way down. I wanted to be enthusiastic, but I just couldn't. I was totally nervous about learning to drive, and the idea of doing it without Mary-Kate by my side made it ten times worse. Plus, Mary-Kate had already been behind the wheel a couple of times with Dad, but I'd never had a chance to try it. She was supposed to help me out. I didn't understand how she could bail on me so easily.

I was about to say something, but she had that far-off look on her face again. Mary-Kate was so obviously happy there was no way I could stay upset. This thing with Jake was really important to her. I sat up again and decided to think positively. I was sure there were plenty of people who took Driver's Ed without their best friend by their side. I was going to be fine—absolutely, totally fine. . . .

chapter seven

I woke up Saturday morning thinking about Driver's Ed. I couldn't believe Mary-Kate bailed on me. But instead of getting angry, I decided to put it out of my mind.

Time to start organizing the guest list for the party! I thought. Just the idea of the party—and having something to organize—made me feel better.

I crawled out of bed on Saturday morning and pulled on my favorite fluffy pink robe. I picked up my purple notebook and pen and opened the door to my bedroom. Across the hall, Mary-Kate opened her door at the very same time. Her hair was sticking out on the right side, and she had a pillow crease across her face. She still looked half asleep.

"I smell French toast," she said with a huge yawn.

I inhaled and realized she was right. My stomach growled when the scent hit my nostrils.

"What are we waiting for then?" I said.

We hurried for the stairs, knocking into each other and laughing as we scurried down to the kitchen. We ran in and took our regular seats at the kitchen table. Mom looked at us over the rim of her coffee cup and smiled.

"Hungry?" she asked.

"How could you tell?" Mary-Kate answered.

"I knew I'd get you up if I made this," Dad said, bringing a plate of steaming hot French toast over to the table.

I grabbed a couple of slices and passed the plate to Mary-Kate. Then I opened up my notebook to a clean page.

"Let's talk guest list," I said, taking a sip of my orange juice. "Who are we going to invite to our party?"

Dad sat down at the head of the table and piled some food on his plate. "Well, Lauren and Brittany, for starters," he said.

"Obviously," I answered. I took a bite of my breakfast and wrote down Lauren and Brittany's names. "Who else?"

"Diana, Marci, and Rachel," Mary-Kate said.

"And we have to invite everyone whose parties we already went to," I added. "That's Tashema, Krista, Melanie, and Sherra."

"Wait a minute," Mom interrupted. She placed

her coffee cup down on the table and turned my notebook toward her so she could scan the list. "These are all girls," she said. "Don't you want to invite some boys, too?"

"Well . . . ," I began, glancing at Mary-Kate. "We haven't actually decided on that yet."

"I don't think we should," Mary-Kate declared. "Boys can be so . . . immature. Plus, some of our friends act different when boys are around. All they think about is who's looking at them, who thinks they look cute, who *they* think looks cute. . . . If we have an all-girl party we'll be more comfortable."

As Mary-Kate made her case, I started to see her point. Our friends weren't the only ones who focused on guys whenever they were around. Mary-Kate and I could be like that, too. Take Todd Malone's party. Mary-Kate had started obsessing about Jake from the moment we got there, and I'd spent half the night trying to find out who that mystery guy—the one I'd hip-checked into the sand—was.

I sighed and thought about his lopsided smile. I wondered, what was he doing right now?

I shook my head. What was wrong with me? I never felt this way about a guy before.

But there was something special about Mystery Guy. . . .

If we *did* have boys at our party, I would love for

him to be my date. But obviously that was never going to happen. I mean, I couldn't even find out what his name was!

"Hey!" Mary-Kate suddenly cried, snapping me out of my thoughts. "We could even make girl power the theme!"

"Girl power . . ." I flipped to our list of possible themes so I could write it down. "I like it. We could have a lot of bright decorations, pictures of strong female characters—"

"Wait a minute!" Mom said. "You don't even have a *theme* yet?"

Mary-Kate and I looked at each other guiltily. "We haven't really had time to nail that one down," Mary-Kate admitted, suddenly becoming very interested in sopping up all the syrup on her plate with her last bit of French toast.

Mom leaned back in her chair and shook her head. "Girls, you'd really better get cracking on some of these bigger things. The party is only six weeks away, and there's a lot of work to do even *after* you send out invitations, pick a theme and a location—"

"Wait!" Mary-Kate yelped. "We've already decided on a location, right, Ashley?"

"Yeah." I smiled at my parents. "We talked about it before bed last night, and we decided we'd like to have the party here . . . at the house."

Mom's face softened. I could tell that she was touched that Mary-Kate and I thought our house was cool enough for the biggest party of our lives.

"Yeah! If we have it here, we can party all night!" Mary-Kate grinned from ear to ear.

"All night?" Dad repeated. "I don't know how the neighbors would feel about that."

Mary-Kate laughed. "I mean, we won't have to end it at a certain time, the way we would if we rented a place out."

Mom and Dad exchanged looks. "What do you think?" she asked. "Want to open our house to a bunch of crazy teenagers?"

"Mom!" Mary-Kate and I blurted in protest.

"I'm kidding!" She raised her hands in surrender. "Of course you girls can have the party here."

"So, back to the boy-girl thing," I said to Mary-Kate. "I understand your point, but are you sure that you want to leave all of our guy friends out? What about—" The phone rang, cutting off my sentence.

"Hello?" Dad answered the phone. Then he glanced at Mary-Kate. "Sure. She's right here." He handed the phone to my sister. "It's Jake."

Mary-Kate's face lit up. She jumped from her seat and grabbed the cordless phone from my father.

"Hi!" she said into the receiver, as she walked into the living room.

I slumped back in my seat, suddenly irritated. Hello? Weren't we in the middle of a discussion here?

"You know what?" I said, staring after Mary-Kate. "I think a girls-only party is a great idea."

"Good," Mom said. She cleared away a few dishes. "Mary-Kate will be happy you decided to go with her plan."

"Let's call Wilson right now and tell him." I picked up my plate and walked it over to the sink.

"Okay. Use my cell phone," Mom offered.

"Thanks, Mom." I grabbed her purse and pulled out her cell, then went back to the table to look up Wilson's number in my notebook.

As I was dialing, I felt nervous. I hoped Wilson liked the idea. And I couldn't wait to tell Mary-Kate that we were going with girl power. She was going to be so psyched . . . *if* she ever got off the phone.

"You've already been out for a run, fed your dog, *and* changed the oil in your Jeep?" I asked Jake, amused.

"Yeah! Why? What have you done this morning?" Jake asked, a laugh in his voice.

"I've . . . uh . . . yawned a lot and eaten some French toast," I admitted. I sat down on the couch and shifted the phone to my other ear.

"Busy girl!" Jake joked.

"Wait!" I said, snapping my fingers. "Ashley and I also started the guest list for our sweet sixteen party."

"Oh, really?" Jake asked, obviously intrigued. "Am I on that guest list?"

I bit the inside of my cheek, remembering something Ashley had said the other day—something about all-girl parties being unsophisticated. If I told Jake that I wanted to invite only girls, he might think I was a big baby.

"I'm . . . not . . . sure," I said, stalling for time.

Jake laughed, obviously taking my answer as a flirty joke instead of the honest truth.

"Well, in that case, I'll just have to spend all my time being nice to you so that you'll decide to invite me," Jake said. "Of course, I was planning on doing that anyway."

My heart melted when he said that. Maybe, just maybe, Ashley was right. Maybe a boy-girl party wasn't such a bad idea. Not if Jake would be my date.

In my mind I saw myself with Jake, walking into the party together hand in hand. Jake looked amazing all dressed up in a suit and tie, and I was wearing that beautiful blue dress Ashley had picked out at the store the other day. We'd dance in the middle of the dance floor while everyone else looked on, sighing over what a perfect couple we were. Somehow, with Jake in the picture, Ashley's sophisticated party plan seemed like the right way to go.

Maybe I'd been a little bit too quick to decide about this all-girl concept. . . .

"I'm really looking forward to seeing you on Monday," Jake said. "Let's meet in the lobby after last period."

"Sounds like a plan!" I agreed.

"Okay," Jake said. "'Bye, Mary-Kate."

"'Bye."

I hung up the phone, and I let out a little squeal of excitement. Then I walked back to the kitchen and found Ashley on Mom's cell.

"Yes, Wilson, we definitely want an all-girl party," she was saying, gripping the phone in one hand as she doodled in her notebook with the other. "And the theme is girl power."

Uh-oh, I thought. *What is she doing?*

Ashley glanced up at me in the middle of a sentence and smiled. She dropped her pen and gave me a little thumbs-up, obviously thinking I was totally thrilled.

"Mary-Kate?" Mom said, a crease of concern on her face. "What's wrong?"

I walked over to the sink where my mother was standing and turned my back to Ashley so she wouldn't be able to hear us.

"It's just . . . I'm kind of surprised that Ashley would call Wilson without me," I said. "I mean, we hadn't *definitely* decided on girl power."

"I thought you'd be pleased," Mom whispered. "I think Ashley really wanted to have boys at your party. It was very thoughtful of her to let you have your way."

Right, I thought. *But it's not my way anymore.* Of course, Ashley had no way of knowing that I was going to change my mind.

"Thanks, Wilson," Ashley said. "'Bye!" She clicked off the phone and turned around in her chair to look at us, a bright smile on her face. "He loves it!" she told us. "He's never done a girl power party before, but he's already got tons of ideas!"

I forced myself to smile. "That's great."

Ashley stood up and gave me a big bear hug. "Isn't this awesome?" she cried, holding onto my shoulders as she pulled away. "We're on our way!"

"Yeah," I said. "It's awesome."

As Ashley grabbed her stuff and headed upstairs to take a shower, I trudged over to the table to clean up my dishes.

My thoughts drifted back to my daydream, then drifted away. In with girl power, out with romance. I just hoped Jake would understand.

chapter eight

Monday afternoon, Ashley and I stood in line at the cafeteria checking out the food. A lunch lady refilled one of the silver steam trays with a grayish substance. She looked up at us and smiled, the steam from the food fogging up her glasses.

"Want to try the meat loaf?" she asked, digging a huge spoon into the mush.

"That's *meat loaf*?" I said, shocked.

We took some macaroni and cheese and inched along toward the cash register. "Listen, I brought a few magazines with me," Ashley told me. "I figured we could go through them for ideas on what to wear to the party."

"Good plan," I agreed. "I don't think the gown-slash-shorts thing is going to work."

"Hey, guys!" Ashley called as she approached our regular table. Brittany, Lauren, Melanie, and Tashema were already there. Everyone said hello as we slid into two empty chairs across from each other.

"We were just talking about going over to Lauren's tonight to watch that *'very special episode'* of *Spencer Academy*," Brittany informed us.

"Yeah. Do you guys want to come?" Lauren asked, taking a bite of her gray meat loaf. I couldn't believe she'd actually ordered that. Brave girl.

"I'm in." Ashley shrugged off her pink sweater and hung it over the back of her chair. "I've been dying to see that episode. Possibly because they've been showing the ads every five seconds for the past week," she added with a laugh.

"Ashley—you promised to help me study for geometry, remember?" I didn't want to burst her *Spencer Academy* bubble, but I definitely needed her help. Geometry isn't exactly my best subject, but Ashley, somehow, totally gets it.

"Oh, right!" Ashley said without even blinking. "Sorry, I forgot. Looks like we're not going to be able to make it, Lauren."

"Thanks, Ashley." I said.

"No problem." Ashley opened her backpack and pulled out a couple of magazines, placing them in the middle of the table. "Okay, I figured we could just go through the fashion spreads and—"

"What's up with this?" Tashema pointed at the magazines with her plastic fork. "We're so boring you need to bring reading material now?"

Everyone laughed as Ashley blushed slightly. "No! We're just going to look for something to wear to our sweet sixteen," she answered. "We went shopping the other day and I picked out a gown . . ."

"And I picked out a shorts and a tank top," I finished, explaining the situation to Tashema and Melanie. "We figure that's not exactly going to work."

"Why don't you go with something in between?" Melanie suggested.

Ashley took a bite of her mac and cheese, thinking it over. "You mean like semiformal? I guess that's an idea."

"Yeah, like really nice pants and some kind of fancy top." Melanie picked up one of the magazines and flipped it open. "Maybe something beaded or sequined. Or you could just wear short dresses instead of long ones."

Melanie was probably the most fashionable of our friends. Her sleek, dark hair was cut in the latest style. Her father's job took him all over the world, and he always brought back the coolest fashions from Paris, Milan, and Tokyo for his only daughter. Ashley and I trusted our own sense of style, but if there was ever a question, we consulted Melanie.

Brittany opened one of the magazines to a fashion spread and held it up. "What about this stuff?"

The picture showed a bunch of girls all dressed up, laughing and talking in a party setting with balloons and streamers. There were a few guys pictured, too, wearing trendy, semicasual suits. One of them even looked a little bit like Jake, and I couldn't help thinking how gorgeous he would look all dressed up.

"Yes, these are perfect!" Melanie exclaimed, taking the magazine out of Brittany's hands and passing it to us. "You guys would look great in that purple dress. Or that red one on the end."

"Oooh! I *love* that!" Ashley said, pointing at the red dress. It had an overlay made out of a black gauzy material and it fell just above the knee, so it wasn't as formal as the gown she had picked out earlier.

"This one's awesome." I showed her a light-blue dress with beaded straps.

"That's perfect for you," Ashley said. "This is a great idea. Everyone likes to get dressed up once in a while."

"Well, girls do, anyway." Tashema leaned over Ashley's shoulder to get a look at the magazine. "But if we wear dresses like that the guys are going to have to wear suits like these guys are . . . or at least nice pants and shirts."

Brittany smirked. "They'll *love* that," she said sarcastically.

"We don't have to worry about the guys," Ashley announced. She snapped the magazine shut and put it back in her bag. "It's going to be an all-girl party."

The second she said it, my face fell. I still had to break the news to Jake. I was looking forward to seeing him that afternoon, but whenever I remembered the conversation we were going to have to have, my stomach twisted into knots.

"Really?" Melanie asked. Her face scrunched up into a confused frown. "Why?"

"Don't sound so disappointed," Brittany said. "We'll live without them."

"Of course we will!" Ashley agreed. "It was Mary-Kate's idea, actually. She just thought it would be more sophisticated without the guys . . . you know . . . being guys."

Don't remind me, I thought, sitting back in my seat and staring at my plate. I couldn't believe that it was all my fault that Jake wasn't going to be at my sweet sixteen—only the biggest night of my life.

"That makes sense," Tashema said. "I think it's a great idea."

"So . . . semiformal dresses?" Ashley asked, raising her eyebrows as she grinned at me.

"Semiformal dresses it is," I agreed. I even managed a convincing smile. "We should start shopping ASAP."

I caught a glimpse of Jake, who was just walk-ing into the cafeteria. My breath caught for a second when I realized he was headed straight for our table.

"Hey, everybody," Jake said when he reached us.

My friends grinned knowingly at each other before calling out, "Hi, Jake!" in unison, then break-ing into giggles.

Jake chuckled as he glanced down at me. "Are they like this all the time?"

"They're all on too much caffeine," I joked.

Yes! A good joke in front of Jake!

"That explains it." Jake shoved his hands into the front pockets of his jeans. "So, my brother and sister are totally excited about meeting you."

Ashley let out a sigh. Jake and I both looked at her as she pushed her macaroni around on her plate. Weird—just two seconds ago she was all excited about dresses. Now she suddenly seemed to be in a bad mood.

"I can't wait to meet them," I told Jake.

"Cool. So what were you guys talking about, anyway?" Jake asked.

"Actually, we were just figuring out some sweet sixteen details," Ashley said, fiddling with the heart pendant she was wearing on a chain around her neck.

I noticed that she barely looked at him when she spoke. Was Ashley nervous around Jake for some reason?

"Oh, the infamous sweet sixteen, huh?" Jake said. "Well, Mary-Kate, I was going to ask you if you wanted to sit with me and my friends, but if you guys are busy . . ."

I felt my face light up at his suggestion. Jake Impenna was asking me to sit at his table! If I went over there, everyone would know we were dating! I looked at my friends and they all grinned back at me, obviously thinking the same thing.

"No, that's okay," I said, standing up. "I'd love to sit with you. Ashley and I can talk later."

"Okay," Jake said. He picked up my tray as I slid out into the aisle between tables. "See you guys later," he said to my friends.

"'Bye, Jake!" they all sing-songed.

"'Bye, guys." I turned to my friends and caught Ashley's eye. She smiled, giving me a little wave. A rush of relief washed through me. Whatever was bothering her couldn't be that big a deal. I'd have to remember to ask her about it later.

When Mary-Kate stood up to go over to Jake's table, I thought I was going to lose it. Here we were talking about our sweet sixteen, and once again she was bailing. And once again it was because of Jake.

This was supposed to be the most important night of our lives, and we hadn't even had much time to talk about it. Didn't she care about the party at all?

"Are you okay?" Lauren asked, glancing at my full plate.

"Oh, I'm fine." I waved my hand. "I wasn't very hungry—and the cafeteria food didn't exactly help."

"Mary-Kate's meeting Jake's brother and sister? I guess he doesn't like her much," Brittany teased. "When is that happening?"

"This afternoon." I leaned my elbows on the table and forced myself to smile.

"Wait a minute," Brittany said, her forehead creasing. "I thought you guys were starting Driver's Ed this afternoon."

I tensed up again. I'd been dreading Driver's Ed all day. That morning I woke up way too early and stared at the ceiling, imagining what it was going to be like to take the course in a strange school where I knew no one. Then I spent most of my time in class wondering if I was going to look like a big loser taking Driver's Ed all by myself.

"Ashley? Are you in there?" Brittany tapped her knuckles on my head. "Are you guys starting the class today or what?"

"We were. I mean, I still am." I shook my head. "But Mary-Kate transferred into the Tuesday/Thursday class." I shrugged as if it wasn't eating me up inside. "So I'm on my own."

Melanie pushed her chair away from the table and looked at me. "Wait a minute. Mary-Kate changed her Driver's Ed class just so she could hang out with some guy for one afternoon?"

"It's not that bad," I insisted. "She's still going to learn to drive. She's just going to do it on different days."

And without me, I added silently.

"Well, it's great that Jake asked her out again so quickly," Tashema said.

"Absolutely!" I said, pulling my food toward me again. "It's fantastic."

And it was . . . kind of.

chapter nine

"**Y**ou are so good with them," I said to Jake. I watched Caitlin and Tristan, his sister and brother, playing together in the park. Eight-year-old Caitlin was pushing five-year-old Tristan on the swings. The four of us had just finished a silly, no-rules basketball game, girls against boys, with ice cream sundaes promised to the winners. Jake and I made sure it ended in a tie.

"Yeah, well, I have the mentality of a five-year-old, so that makes it easy," Jake explained. "What's your excuse?"

"Well, I'd say I'm about eight, so I guess that's why I bonded with Caitlin," I deadpanned.

"I'll make sure she invites you to her next slumber party," Jake joked.

"I am *so* there," I said. "I've been looking for a reason to break out my Snoopy sleeping bag."

Jake bounced the basketball in front of him.

"Speaking of parties . . . have I locked in an invitation to your sweet sixteen yet?"

All the blood rushed out of my face. How could I tell him he wasn't invited? *Think, Mary-Kate!* I told myself. *Think!* But I didn't come up with much.

"Yeah," I said finally. "I mean . . . yes, of course you're invited."

"Great." Jake gave me a wide smile. "I knew you'd come around."

I laughed, my pulse racing. So I'd gone with my heart. So what? Ashley had always *wanted* boys at the party, I told myself. I was sure I could get her to change her mind again with no problem.

"You're late," a not-so-kind-looking lady barked at me as I hurried into the Driver's Ed classroom. She had frizzy brown hair and crooked glasses. She stood at the front of the room with the name "Ms. Junger" scrawled on the board behind her. She was my Driver's Ed teacher. "What's your name?"

"I'm Ashley." I flashed her an apologetic smile. "I'm sorry I'm late." Mom and I had gotten stuck in traffic on the way to Columbus High, where I was taking the class.

"Don't let it happen again," Ms. Junger snapped. She nodded at the only empty desk, right smack in the middle of the front row. "Have a seat."

I swallowed hard and made my way over to the

chair, feeling everyone's eyes on me as I slid into it. Some of the kids already had bright yellow books on their desks. I really was late.

"As I was just about to explain," Ms. Junger said, looking down her nose at me, "we don't have enough books to go around, so you're going to have to share."

I gazed around to see if anyone was partnerless, but it seemed as if everyone had a friend. Finally, I glanced to the right and caught the eye of the guy sitting next to me. I froze. It was *the guy*! The mystery guy from Todd Malone's party!

"You!" he exclaimed, with his lopsided grin.

"You!" I said right back.

I was about to ask him if he had a partner when the teacher announced that she was going to call the roll. She read a list of names, and I sat back in my chair, waiting until she got to my mystery guy. I was finally going to find out his name! The afternoon was suddenly looking up.

"Ben Jones?" Ms. Junger called out. Mystery Guy raised his hand, and I tried not to smile. Ben Jones. Nice name.

When she was done, I looked at Ben again, ready to ask him if he wanted to share a book, but he was already pulling his desk over to a boy on his other side. I frowned, disappointed. So much for me getting to know the mystery guy.

Meanwhile, I still didn't have a book, and Ms. Junger was about to start class.

"Do you have a partner?" a voice asked behind me.

I turned around and my eyes fell on a nice-looking guy who was behind me to my left. He had buzz-cut brown hair and wore a Star Wars T-shirt. But most important, he had his own book. He held it up in front of him and smiled.

"You can share with me if you want," he whispered. "I'm Evan."

"Thanks," I responded. "I'm Ashley."

Ms. Junger started with chapter one—"All About Safety." Taking a deep breath, I told myself, once again, that everything was going to be fine. It couldn't get much worse.

Then Evan let out the loudest sneeze I've ever heard. Everyone in the room laughed, and Evan sniffled loudly. Ben turned around to look at us, and when he caught my eye, he smiled. I almost melted. Could he *be* any cuter?

"Sorry," Evan said. "Bad cold."

"Just try to keep it down," Ms. Junger told him.

From that point on, Evan did nothing but sniffle, sneeze, and blow his nose. I felt bad for him, of course, but it was no fun sitting right next to him while he made all that noise. It was hard to pay attention to what Ms. Junger was saying. Toward the end of the class, the teacher decided to go over everything she'd lectured on. She picked up her book and walked to the front of her desk, leaning back against it.

"What's the first thing you should do when you sit down in your car?" she asked.

A few hands went up, and she called on a red-headed girl. "Janine?"

"Put on your seat belt and check your mirrors," Janine answered.

"Right," Ms. Junger said, glancing down at her book again. "How far from a corner should you be when you turn on your signal indicating that you intend to turn?"

I raised my hand, but Ms. Junger called on someone else. At that point, Evan started to blow his nose again. This time it was so loud, all the people around us either turned to look, or started to shift uncomfortably in their chairs. I leaned slightly to the right to avoid getting sneezed on. I didn't want him to think I was trying to get away from him, but I couldn't help it. I didn't want to get sick.

I watched as he crumbled up the tissue and stuffed it in the back pocket of his backpack with a bunch of others. I wrinkled my nose and turned away. Ugh! Colds could be so icky. . . .

"Ashley?"

I sat up straight when I heard my name. Ms.

Junger was staring right at me, and she did not look pleased.

"Are you going to answer my question?" she demanded, crossing her arms over her chest.

Question? What question? I hadn't even heard the answer to the last one. "Ummm . . ." What was I supposed to say? I had to answer something, or she'd know that I wasn't paying attention.

Think! I told myself. *What would be the next logical question after the blinker thing?* I looked at my book. The topic right after signaling was stopping. Maybe she'd asked how long you're supposed to wait at a stop sign. I took a stab in the dark.

"Five seconds?" I said, raising my eyebrows with hope.

The whole classroom burst out laughing. I wanted to sink into the floor.

"Very good, Ashley." Ms. Junger smirked. "That's exactly the amount of practice time you have to spend behind the wheel before they'll test you for your license. Five whole seconds."

Everyone laughed even harder. I glanced over at Ben, who was practically falling out of his chair. Why did this have to happen to me?

I stared down at the book, wishing Ms. Junger would move on to the next question. Where was Mary-Kate when I needed her? She always knows exactly what to say to make awkward situations better. She would definitely be cracking some perfect joke right now——something that would make everyone forget my lame answer.

When I looked up at Ben again, he was gazing at me sympathetically. I managed to crack a small smile. At least I'd finally found my mystery guy. And now that I knew who he was, Driver's Ed was going to be a whole lot more fun!

chapter ten

"Ashley, I can't believe she actually said that to you!" I exclaimed, flopping back in my chair at the dinner table. "A whole five seconds,'" I repeated, mimicking Ashley's imitation of Ms. Junger. "I hope I have a different teacher."

"For your sake, I hope so, too." Ashley glanced up from her plate and half smiled. "Anyway . . . I've been thinking about our sweet sixteen, and I have an idea. What if we rent a karaoke machine? We could do a whole divas thing, you know? Everyone's going to be all dressed up, and we can take turns belting out girl power songs to go with our theme."

"Girl power songs?" Dad repeated. "Like what?"

"You know, like 'I Will Survive,' 'R-E-S-P-E-C-T,' 'Survivor.' Stuff like that," Ashley said. "What do you think, Mary-Kate?"

Now's your chance, I thought. *Tell her you want to have boys at the party before she comes up with a ten-mile-long list of girl power songs.*

"Karaoke would be great!" I said brightly. "And our invitations are perfect for it." I paused, searching for a smooth way to bring boys into the conversation. Karaoke . . . boys . . . karaoke . . .boys . . .

"Hey! You know what would be *so* funny?" I began, trying to seem casual. "If our guy friends had to sing karaoke."

Ashley scrunched up her nose. "Yeah . . . I guess that would be funny."

"I mean, imagine Todd trying to sing some Glowstick song," I said, laughing awkwardly. "Or Mike and Brian doing those hip-hop songs they love to imitate."

Come on, Ash, I thought, holding my breath. *Take the hint.*

Ashley giggled and pushed her hair behind her ears. "Ugh! Thank God we're not having guys there," she said. "I don't think I could handle Mike and Brian in stereo surround sound. They're bad enough when they do that routine in the lunchroom."

"Yeah," I said slowly. "Thank God."

Okay, so that didn't work. I took a sip of water and waited for another opportunity.

"So, you decided to go dressy, huh?" Mom noted as she helped herself to more salad.

"Yep." Ashley nodded. "Mary-Kate and I saw a

few things in my magazines that would be perfect."

"You know, it's actually almost too bad we don't have guys coming," I chimed in, twirling a few strands of hair around my finger.

"What do you mean?" Ashley asked.

"Wouldn't you love to see them all dressed up?" I asked, appealing to Ashley's cute-boy-loving side. "They never wear anything but jeans and sweats."

Ashley shifted in her seat, staring at me uncertainly. "Yeah, but—"

"And imagine the torture it would be for them, having to wear those fancy suits!" I exclaimed. "It would be worth it just to see some of them squirm."

"Yeah," Ashley said. "But I really think we were right with this all-girls thing. We're going to have a great time. Besides, the guys *would* be squirming the whole time, and if they were miserable, we'd all be miserable."

"Mary-Kate, you've already decided on a girl power theme, and you've gotten the ball rolling," Mom said. "There's no need to go back on that now."

"I know," I admitted. "I didn't want to *change* it, I was just saying it would be funny . . . you know . . . to see the guys dressed up. That's all."

Mom pushed her chair away from the table. "Good. It's all settled then."

"You two are going to have a great party," Dad put

in, picking up a few dishes as he rose from the table.

"Yeah. We definitely are." I tried to sound enthusiastic as I got up to help.

But my whole body felt heavy as I carried a couple of the serving dishes around the table. I couldn't believe Ashley was clinging so hard to the all-girls idea. Convincing her should have been a snap.

Getting her to change her mind was obviously going to be tougher than I'd thought, but I had to do it.

I had to.

After dinner, our parents went up to their room, and I followed Mary-Kate into the living room to start our geometry study session.

"So . . . ready to study?" I asked.

"Oh! I forgot to tell you," Mary-Kate said, grabbing her bag from the floor by the front door. "Jake's coming over to help me study tonight."

I crossed my arms over my chest. "When did you decide this?" I felt like I'd just been punched in the stomach. She couldn't be serious.

"This afternoon on our way back from the park." Mary-Kate's grin faded a bit. "I told him that I was stressed out about the test, and he offered to tutor me. I figured you'd be happy not to have to work tonight."

I took a deep breath and let it out slowly, trying not to get overly annoyed. "Mary-Kate, I *planned* to help you tonight," I said. "I could have gone over to Lauren's, remember?"

"I'm sorry!" Mary-Kate said as she pulled a couple of books out of her bag. "I wouldn't have said yes if I knew you were going to be mad. I thought you'd be relieved that you didn't have to help me with geometry *again.*"

I held Mary-Kate's gaze for a moment longer, but I felt my anger wavering. She probably did think she was doing me a favor by taking Jake up on his offer. It just irritated me that I was being brushed aside for Jake for the second time that day. The third time if you counted the whole Driver's Ed thing.

"I'm sorry, okay?" Mary-Kate said sincerely.

"It's okay," I said with a sigh. "I guess I'll just watch *Spencer Academy* while you guys work."

At that moment the doorbell rang, and Mary-Kate grinned. "That's him!" she cried giddily. "Do I look okay?"

"You look great," I told her.

She bounded across the room and opened the door. Jake was standing on the front step, and his whole face lit up when he saw Mary-Kate. I couldn't help feeling happy for my sister. If Jake was looking at her like that, he definitely had it as bad as she did.

"Hey, Mary-Kate. Hey, Ashley." He nodded at me.

"Hi, Jake! Come on in." Mary-Kate led him into the living room.

"So I hear you're relieving me of my tutoring duties," I said to Jake, shoving my hands in the back pockets of my jeans as we all walked into the living room together. "I guess I should thank you."

"No problem," Jake said. He adjusted the strap of his backpack on his shoulder. "I actually kind of liked the class. Don't tell anyone, though."

"He's obviously insane," Mary-Kate joked, prompting a laugh from Jake.

We all turned when we heard somebody on the stairs. "You must be Jake," Dad said as he walked into the room. He didn't seem surprised to see a guy in the living room, so I assumed Mary-Kate had told my parents he was coming over.

"Hi! It's nice to meet you," Jake said, reaching over to shake hands.

"You, too." Dad smiled approvingly at Mary-Kate, obviously happy to find that Jake was so polite.

"Well, I guess we should just get this over with," Mary-Kate said, clearing a few magazines off the coffee table as Jake settled down on the couch.

I felt my shoulders tense up as he opened his bag and pulled out his old notebook. "Wait a minute," I said. "You guys are going to study in here?"

"Yeah . . . why?" Mary-Kate said.

"I was going to watch *Spencer Academy*," I said, hating the whiny sound of my voice. I cleared my throat and lifted my chin. "I mean, can't you guys study in mom's office or something so I can have the big-screen TV?"

"Ashley." Dad came up behind me and rested his hands on my shoulders. "It's a lot more comfortable for two people in here. You can watch your show up in your room."

My skin grew warm from embarrassment as I stood there, basically being scolded by my father in front of Mary-Kate and her new boyfriend.

"Fine." I threw my hands up and let them slap back down against my jeans.

Before anyone could say anything else to me, I turned and took the steps two at a time. I couldn't believe the way this night had turned out. First I bailed on Lauren and my other friends to help Mary-Kate, who basically tossed me aside. Now I was getting kicked out of my own living room. It was so unfair!

I walked into my bedroom and closed the door behind me. Flopping down on my bed, I grabbed my remote and flicked on my tiny portable TV. *Spencer Academy* hadn't started yet.

The phone rang, and I reached over to my nightstand to answer it.

"Hello, this is Wilson Miller," a voice said on the other line. I could hear hip-hop music playing in the background. "I'd like to speak to Ashley or Mary-Kate, please."

"Hi, Wilson, it's Ashley," I said. "What's up? Where are you calling from?"

"I'm at video shoot in Aspen," he explained. "But I wanted to check in with you. How are your party plans coming?"

"Well, I was thinking about getting a karaoke machine and trying to find tapes full of girl power songs," I told him. "What do you think?"

"That's a fabulous idea!" Wilson said. "Really. A great touch, Ashley. I think you have a knack for this stuff."

"Thanks." The compliment from Wilson made me flush happily.

"Now, how about the guest list?" he asked. "I really need it, Ashley. I thought you'd have e-mailed it to me by now."

I glanced across the room at my purple notebook on my desk and thought about our breakfast guest list conversation. Mary-Kate and I hadn't gotten very far that morning before Jake had called. The list wasn't remotely ready to send out yet.

"We're . . . working on it," I said slowly.

"We've got to get those invitations out A.S.A.P.," Wilson urged. "The party's less than six weeks away! I need the guest list by the time I get back from Aspen."

Great, I thought. *Like I'm ever going to find more than five minutes alone with Mary-Kate to figure it all out.* But I wasn't going to say that to Wilson.

"No problem," I said breezily.

"Good!" Wilson said. "I'll be back in two days. Talk to you then."

"Okay! Thanks, Wilson!"

I clicked off the phone and sat still for a moment, staring at my desk. Downstairs, Mary-Kate let out a peal of laughter. I sighed. If she kept spending all her time with Jake, we would never get the guest list done. And I, for one, wanted to make sure this party went off with out a hitch.

I got up and grabbed my notebook, a pen, and my address book. Then I climbed back onto my bed, flipped the notebook open to the list of names we'd begun on Saturday, and started looking up addresses.

I never expected to be working on our sweet sixteen alone. But someone had to do it. And it obviously wasn't going to be Mary-Kate. I couldn't help feeling like our sweet sixteen was taking a backseat to Jake.

"Well, if that's the way she wants it, that's fine

by me," I said aloud. I heard her laugh again, and I turned up the volume on my little TV to drown the sound out.

Apparently, I was going to have to start making decisions about this party by myself.

chapter eleven

"**I**'ve never been this nervous in my life," I told Janine, the red-headed girl from my Driver's Ed class.

We were standing in front of Columbus High on Wednesday afternoon with my mystery guy, Ben Jones, waiting for Ms. Junger to pull the student driver car around.

We watched as a little white car wound through the parking lot and stopped in front of us. There was a huge red sign on the roof that read: "Columbus Driving School—Student Driver!"

"Why doesn't it just say 'Danger! Idiot behind the wheel!'" Ben joked.

Janine and I laughed as Ms. Junger got out of the car. She flashed us her now familiar glare.

"Driving is no laughing matter, people," she said. Then she looked down at her clipboard and held out the keys in front of us. My heart pounded just looking at them. This was really happening! I was really going to learn to drive!

"Let's see . . . who's going first?" Ms. Junger muttered to herself.

I glanced at Ben and Janine, who both looked as scared as I felt. *Don't pick me*, I thought. *Just don't pick me!*

"Ashley?" Ms. Junger said. "Get behind the wheel."

She slapped the keys into my hand, and my legs instantly turned to Jell-O. Then she walked over to the passenger side door. "Let's get going!"

"You'll be fine," Janine said when she saw me hesitating. "We're all in this together."

Ben opened the door to the backseat and let Janine slide in before him. "Don't worry," he said, his deep brown eyes reassuring. "You're going to do great."

I slipped into the driver's seat and closed the door. Then I glanced at Ms. Junger for direction.

"What's the first thing you do?" she barked.

First thing, first thing . . . How was I supposed to be able to remember our lesson when I was shaking so hard?

"Seat belt and mirrors!" I cried. I pulled the seat belt on and snapped it into the buckle, then adjusted the rearview mirror.

"Okay, now put the key in the ignition and your

right foot on the brake pedal," Ms. Junger ordered.

I did as she said, started up the engine, and clasped the steering wheel so hard my knuckles turned white.

"Now, put on your left blinker, check your mirror for traffic, and slowly pull out," Ms. Junger instructed.

Here goes nothing, I thought.

Ever so carefully, I picked my foot up off the brake and pushed down on the gas pedal. Suddenly, we flew forward, and I let out a little squeal. I heard Janine shriek from the backseat, but Ben just laughed.

"Brake!" Ms. Junger yelled.

I slammed on the brake, and we all jerked forward. My seat belt cut into my chest as I gasped for breath, my hair blanketing my face.

"I said slowly," Ms. Junger growled through her teeth.

"Sorry," I said. "I've never done this before."

Ms. Junger took an audible breath in through her nose and let it out slowly. "It's okay. It happens to everyone."

Hey! That was the first nice thing I ever heard the woman say.

"Let's try it again," she prompted.

This time, I pressed gently on the gas pedal, and we moved slowly through the parking lot. By the time I got to the exit, I was calming down a bit. It just took a little while to get a feel for the power of the gas and the brake.

Ms. Junger instructed me to make a right turn. I looked both ways, then turned the wheel. Suddenly, we were driving on the wrong side of the street! Luckily, the school was on a quiet back road, so there were no other cars around. Ms. Junger reached out and gently turned the wheel further to the right.

"There you go," Ms. Junger said. "Now go up to that stop sign—slowly—and try it again."

I jerked the car only a little coming to a stop, then I turned on my blinker.

"Hey! We're turning on to my street," Ben said. "That's my house right on the corner."

I glanced up at the big blue house he was pointing to. Then I hit the gas, cutting the wheel more this time, and before I knew what was happening, we were flying straight for the curb . . . and a big black mailbox!

"Brake!" Ms. Junger shouted.

I slammed my foot down hard. I let out a shriek as the car jumped the curb and plowed right over the mailbox. *Ben's* mailbox.

I slowly turned to look at Ms. Junger. "Sorry."

The instructor had her hands braced on the dashboard. Ben clutched his stomach and laughed like a hyena in the backseat and Janine turned white. My foot was still pressed hard into the brake, and I was afraid to move a muscle. I couldn't believe I had an accident on my very first day of driving!

Ms. Junger gritted her teeth. "Just put it in reverse and pull back out."

My eyes filled up with tears as I reached for the gear shift, but I managed to get back out onto the road. I put the car in park, and we all climbed out to assess the damage.

It was pretty bad. Ben's mailbox was lying on its side, all dented. Ms. Junger left the three of us by the car and went up to his house to apologize for the accident.

"Are you okay?" I asked Janine.

"Oh, I'm fine," she answered with a wave of her hand. She was still pale, but she seemed to be handling it well.

"Ben, I am *so* sorry," I said. "Really. I'll pay for it . . . somehow."

Ben finally stopped laughing and looked at me, his eyes glimmering. "Geez, Ashley. Ever thought of trying out for the demolition derby?"

"No." I crossed my arms over my chest. "But maybe you should consider calling Bad Jokes Anonymous."

Ben blinked, obviously taken aback. But then he smirked, impressed. I couldn't believe it myself.

Wow! I actually thought of a comeback at the exact moment I needed it instead of two days later! Mary-Kate would have been so proud.

Ms. Junger returned and instructed Ben to get behind the wheel.

By the time we got back to the school, Ben and Janine had both had their turns behind the wheel and had done well. Ms. Junger dropped us off at the school, and we all walked inside, chatting happily.

Ben swung open the door. "Well, that was . . . interesting."

"And fun," Janine added. "If I had to go through that with someone, I'm glad it was you guys."

"Thanks." I smiled. "I'm glad it was you guys, too."

"Hey! You know what?" Janine said, coming to a stop in front of our classroom. "I'm having this party on my dad's boat on Friday night. You two should come."

I hesitated for a moment. What about Mary-Kate? We always went to parties together. Maybe she would want to come along. Then I realized she probably had plans with Jake for the weekend. So why shouldn't I make some plans of my own?

"I'd love to," I told Janine.

"Me, too." Ben glanced at me. "In fact, I'll pick you up if you want." He shrugged. "I mean, my parents and I will . . . you know."

"Do you really think they're going to want to drive the girl who leveled their mailbox?" I asked, raising my eyebrows.

"They're very forgiving people," Ben assured me.

"This is great!" Janine exclaimed, clapping her hands. "It's like a date!"

I grinned and stared straight into Ben's deep brown eyes. "Is that what it is?" I asked. "A date?"

Ben rubbed at the back of his neck. "Sure! I mean, yeah. If that's okay with you."

"That is *definitely* okay with me," I told him.

Wednesday evening, Jake was driving me home in his Jeep after a whole afternoon of studying and swimming.

Now we zipped through the streets with the top down, blaring our favorite radio station on the stereo. I had my sunglasses on, the wind was whipping through my hair, and with the cutest guy in school behind the wheel, I'd never felt so cool in my life. Too bad we couldn't drive by the houses of every single person I knew!

"Thanks again for helping me with geometry," I shouted to Jake over the radio. "I really think I'm picking it up."

Jake smiled. "Believe it or not, I had fun."

"Yeah, right," I said.

But I knew he was telling the truth. The past

couple of times we'd gotten together really *had* been fun, even though we were studying. Jake was constantly making me laugh. And somehow it really helped me remember things.

"Well, you can reward me for all my trouble by dancing with me at your sweet sixteen," Jake said as he turned onto my block.

My stomach dropped. I had to make Ashley change her mind about the party, and fast! The longer I waited to straighten this all out, the more I felt like I was lying to Jake *and* Ashley.

Jake dropped me off. I gave him a quick kiss, then jogged into the house. As I slammed the door behind me, I decided that it was time to take the direct approach. That has always been my style, after all.

Outside Ashley's closed bedroom door, I paused and took a deep breath, planning what I was going to say. Then I knocked and opened the door. Ashley was sitting at her desk doing her homework. Her music was so loud she didn't even hear me walk in.

"Hey, Ashley!" I shouted.

She flinched and put her hand over her heart. "You scared me!" She laughed.

"Sorry!" I crossed the room to turn her music down a bit. "I need to talk to you."

Ashley turned in her chair, resting her arm on the back. "Everything okay?"

"Yeah. Everything's fine." I perched on the edge of her bed and crossed my legs, then uncrossed them and leaned back on my hands. Why was I so fidgety?

"Listen, I've been thinking about this whole girls-only thing," I said, finally sitting up straight. "And I've changed my mind. I think we should invite guys to our party."

There was a long moment of silence, and it hung in the air like a dark cloud. Ashley's face tightened. She looked shocked—*angry* and shocked.

"You *have* to be kidding me!" she shouted, jumping to her feet so fast her chair almost tipped over. She caught it just in time and glared at me. "You haven't been involved with the party planning at all and *now* you're springing this on me?"

"Wait a minute," I protested, standing. "What do you mean I haven't been involved at all?"

"All you've been thinking about for the past week is Jake, Jake, Jake," Ashley complained, tilting her head back and forth each time she said his name. "You spend every second with him, and we've barely had a chance to talk about the party."

My mouth fell open. I was stunned by Ashley's reaction. After all, hadn't we made a guest list together? Hadn't we decided on dresses together? And I knew I had been in on the whole karaoke conversation.

"I'm sorry, Mary-Kate," Ashley said, sitting down again. She picked up her pen and deliberately turned her back on me. "There is no way I'm going to change the party now. Not after all the work I've done."

"Ashley, you don't understand." I tried to stay calm so I could explain. I moved to the side of her chair to try to get her to look at me. "When Jake and I were at the park the other day—"

Ashley interrupted me. "You know what? It doesn't matter anyway. I already finished the guest list, complete with addresses, *on my own,* and sent it to Wilson. And every guest on that list is a girl, so there's no turning back now."

"You *what?*" I blurted. "How could you do that without showing it to me? Or even *telling* me anything about it?"

"Well, I'm sorry," Ashley said sarcastically, slapping her pen down on the desk and finally looking up at me. "But if you hadn't been so busy with Jake I would have asked for your help."

"I know why you're doing this," I said. "You just don't want to change the party because I have a boyfriend and you don't."

Ashley pulled back as if she'd been slapped. Then her eyes narrowed into little slits, and she stood up to face me.

"I can't believe you just said that," Ashley said,

her voice cracking. "Can you please just leave?"

I just stood there for a moment, unsure of what to do. She'd never thrown me out of her room before.

"I'm serious, Mary-Kate," she warned, her voice growing louder. "Leave me alone."

"Fine!" I said. I turned on my heel and stormed out of her room, slamming the door behind me.

Two seconds later she turned her music back on, even louder this time. I stood outside her door and listened, my eyes filling with tears. Ashley and I had never had a fight this big before. And I don't think either one of us had ever said such hurtful things to the other.

I wiped my eyes and walked back to my room, wondering if things were ever going to be the same between Ashley and me again.

chapter twelve

That night at dinner I couldn't even look at Mary-Kate, let alone talk to her. The silence was definitely driving my parents insane.

"So, Ashley," Mom said to me, fiddling with her earring. "Didn't you have your first turn behind the wheel today?"

I sighed loudly, pushing my rice around on my plate. "Yep."

I glanced at Mary-Kate. There was so much I wanted to tell her about—my driving lesson, the comeback I'd flung at Ben, and my new friend Janine and her party. And about the fact that I had a date, an actual *date* with the amazingly cute mystery guy from Todd Malone's party.

But that obviously wasn't going to happen.

"What about you, Mary-Kate?" Mom prompted, turning toward my sister. "How was your afternoon?"

"Well, I'd tell you, Mom, but I don't think *some* people at the table want to hear about Jake anymore."

"Ooookay." Dad took a long sip of water and studied each of us, running his hand over his slightly shaggy brown hair.

"What about your party?" he asked. "How's the planning going?"

"I don't want to talk about it," Mary-Kate and I said at the exact same time, in the same annoyed tone.

I scowled at her and she scowled right back. I looked down at the table and felt like crying. At that moment I couldn't even imagine celebrating our birthday together.

"Can I be excused?" I asked, pulling my napkin off my lap.

"Ashley, you've barely touched your dinner," Mom said.

I knew she hated it when Mary-Kate and I were upset with each other. "Maybe I'll eat it later," I said.

"Well . . . okay, sweetie," she said. "You can go."

I stood up slowly and walked out of the dining room. And even though I could feel Mary-Kate watching me, I didn't look back.

"Okay, Mary-Kate, you're doing fine," Ms. Junger said. "Please pull to the next stop sign and make a right."

It was Thursday afternoon, and I was taking my first turn behind the wheel. Ashley was right—Ms. Junger was definitely strict. I gripped the wheel tightly and followed Ms. Junger's instructions. Two girls I didn't know chattered away in the back seat.

I drove to the stop sign, and carefully looked left and right. I turned the wheel while lightly pressing down on the gas when I saw that no one was coming.

"Just continue down this road," Ms. Junger requested.

My shoulders relaxed a bit. Driving in a straight line? I could handle that. I steered the car and kept a slow but constant speed.

As I stared at the road ahead, I found myself thinking about Ashley's accusation—that I had been spending all my time with Jake and not helping her with the party.

It's true, I realized as I remembered all the hours I had spent with Jake this week. *Ashley is right. I haven't been helping with the party at all.*

"Stop sign, Mary-Kate! Stop sign!"

"What?" I stomped down on the brake. Too late!

The car's tires squealed on the pavement. The girls in the backseat screamed as we drove right past the bright red sign and through a four-way intersection.

The car skidded to the other side of the intersection and stopped. I struggled to catch my breath. "Is everyone okay?" I asked.

Luckily, I hadn't done any serious damage.

I turned to Ms. Junger. Her eyes were squeezed shut, and I swear I heard her mutter, "Just like her sister."

"Pull over, Mary-Kate," she said. "I think it's Monica's turn to drive now."

I felt like a total moron. My legs shook as I got out of the car and switched places with Monica. But as soon as I settled into the backseat, I started thinking about Ashley again, trying to see things from her point of view. I *had* been spending a lot of time with Jake lately. And the other day, when we were making up the guest list, I *had* ditched her to talk on the phone with him. Plus I did bail on her at lunch when we were talking about dresses.

I swallowed hard and looked out the window as Monica lurched the car around a corner. A wave of guilt washed over me. I hugged myself and sighed.

I'm going to have to un-invite Jake, I realized. It was the only way Ashley and I were ever going to be friends again.

"Hey, Mary-Kate!" Jake called as I wove my way through the crowded school hallway the next afternoon.

"Hey!" I said brightly.

110

Jake's eyes narrowed and he put his hands in the pockets of his varsity jacket. "Everything okay?"

"Funny you should ask," I replied. One of the benches by the wall was empty and I gestured toward it. "Want to sit?"

"Uh-oh." Jake gave a little nervous laugh. "This does not sound good."

I put my hand on his arm. I realized it must have sounded like I was going to dump him or something.

"It's about my party," I explained, taking a seat.

I paused to take a deep breath and told myself to just do it. Quick and painless, like ripping off a Band-Aid. Although, whatever people told you, that Band-Aid thing usually hurt.

"I don't know how to say this, so I'm just gonna say it," I began. "I'm sorry but I can't invite you to my sweet sixteen."

"Oh," he said, obviously confused. "That's . . . ummm . . . why not?"

"Ashley and I had decided to have an all-girl party, but I really wanted to invite you, so I did. I figured I'd be able to change her mind—"

"But you couldn't," Jake finished.

"Right," I said, scrunching my nose. "We had a big fight, actually. I would keep trying to convince her, but I think I need to let it go, you know? It's the only way we're going to make up."

"That's okay," Jake said. "I understand. But I want to take you out for your birthday, if that's okay. You know, on another night."

I reached out to hold his hand. "I'd love that."

Then, before I even knew what was happening, Jake was leaning in to kiss me. My whole body tingled with nervousness, but I managed to tilt my head and close my eyes just in time.

Our lips met, and it was as though everything around us disappeared. The kiss was long and slow and totally amazing—I wanted it to go on forever. Now I knew what people meant when they talked about a *real* kiss!

That night when Jake dropped me off, I ran right into the house and bounded up the steps to Ashley's room. I couldn't wait to talk to her and get everything straightened out. I knocked and walked in, but she wasn't there.

Disappointed, I went back downstairs and found my parents snuggled together on the couch in the living room, watching the evening news.

"Where's Ashley?" I asked, resting on the arm of the comfy chair.

"She went out to a party," Mom told me.

"A party?" I repeated, stunned.

I felt all the blood rush out of my face as I tried to process what Mom was saying. What? Ashley went to a party and she didn't even tell me about it?

"Yes." Mom pulled away from Dad slightly so she could see me better. "I'm surprised you didn't know. She's been talking about it for the last two days."

"Whose party was it?" I asked, slowly sliding off the arm of the chair and into the seat. I hadn't heard about any parties at school. Usually, if one of us is invited to something, the other one is, too.

"It's at her friend Janine's house," Mom answered. "She really didn't tell you?"

"No," I replied with a shrug. I didn't even know Ashley had a friend named Janine.

"Did you guys drop her off?" I asked, wondering if maybe this Janine girl was from another town or something.

"No, actually," Dad said, stretching his arms out and yawning. "A boy came by with his parents to pick her up. Ben was his name. Nice kid."

"Excuse me?" I blurted. "She had a *date*?" My brain was reeling. Ashley had friends I'd never heard of. She had a date she'd never even said a word to me about!

"Um, Mom?" I said, toying with the hem on my sweater. "Do you happen to know where Ashley met Ben?"

"He's a friend of hers from her Driver's Ed class," Mom answered. "She said something about bumping into him at Todd's party and then he ended up being in her class. That's where she met Janine, too."

"Oh," I said.

Driver's Ed. That made sense.

"I knew you girls were fighting on Wednesday, but I was hoping you'd made up by now," Mom said.

"Don't worry about it, Mom." I didn't want to worry her. "It's no big deal."

But it was a big deal. It was a *tremendous* deal. Ashley had new friends and a new guy to date and a party to go to in some totally different town with different people. And I wasn't a part of it. I didn't even know anything about it.

A feeling of dread seeped into my chest. Ashley was right. I *had* been neglecting her in favor of Jake. Not just the party, but *her.* My sister. My best friend in the whole world.

chapter thirteen

"Watch your step, Ashley," Ben teased, his dark eyes shining. "And whatever you do, don't knock me over."

"Look out," I joked. "I'm a one-woman safety hazard."

Ben smiled. He held out his hand to help me from the pier to Janine's father's sleek white boat. "This place is so beautiful," I gushed.

"Definitely cool," Ben agreed.

He held on to my hand after I'd safely made it to the deck. I didn't want him to let go. I was *so* attracted to this guy. I couldn't believe I was finally on a date with him!

"Hey, guys!" Janine called. "I'm so glad you came."

Janine had set up tables of snacks and drinks on the deck of the boat, but most of the party was actually taking place on the picr itsclf. Little white lights were strung from the lampposts that lined either side of the long wooden pier. A sound system on the bow blasted one of the local pop stations.

There were dozens of people milling around, talking and laughing.

She poured two Cokes and handed them to us.

"Thanks for inviting us," I said.

"Well, just make yourselves at home. The pier is all ours tonight."

"Janine! Come here! I can't find the plates!" one of her friends shouted from down below.

"Sorry, I'll catch up with you later," Janine said with an apologetic smile.

"So—do you want to walk down to the end of the pier and check out the view?" Ben asked.

I took a sip of my soda. "Don't you want to mingle?"

"Nah. I'm totally antisocial."

We climbed off the boat, then moved together through the crowd. We walked out to the end of the pier, where we were entirely alone. I leaned against the railing and gazed out across the ocean to the moonlit spot where the water met the sky. I sighed. It didn't get better than this. Beautiful night. Great party. Gorgeous boy . . .

"I'm really glad you came to the party with me tonight," Ben whispered.

"Me, too," I said, my heart pounding.

All I wanted at that moment was for him to kiss me.

Then he leaned in. I closed my eyes. . .

When our lips met, it felt as if the pier was moving below my feet. I couldn't have imagined a more amazing kiss. When we parted, Ben's eyes were still closed, and I smiled. Apparently he'd thought it was amazing, too.

"Wow," he said.

"Yeah," I said, biting my bottom lip. "Wow."

We moved over and sat down on the bench, which was good because my knees were so weak I probably couldn't have stood for much longer.

Now I understood how Mary-Kate felt about Jake—and why she tried to change our sweet sixteen plans. She didn't want to spend her birthday without him.

"What are you thinking about?" Ben asked.

"I'm thinking I'd like to invite you to my sweet sixteen." I smiled. "Want to be my date?"

Ben flashed his lopsided grin. "I'd love to," he said. "As long as there are no party hats involved because, you know, I have a rep to protect."

"No party hats." I laughed. "I swear."

"Then I'm in," Ben said. He reached out and took my hand again, lacing my fingers through his. "Thanks for asking."

"Thanks for saying yes," I answered.

I was so ridiculously happy at that moment, part of me wished the night would never end. But another part—a big part—couldn't wait to get home to tell Mary-Kate the good news. The boy-girl party was back on, and now we *both* had dates!

"Mary-Kate, are you awake?" Ashley whispered late on Friday night. I heard her come in after her party and was hoping she'd stop by my room! It was way past time to apologize.

"Come on in," I said, sitting up.

Ashley flicked on my bedside lamp as she sat down on the edge of my mattress.

"I'm sorry!" we both said at the exact same time.

"You're sorry?" we both said again.

Then we both laughed. It felt as if a huge weight was being lifted off my shoulders.

"I'm really sorry for being such a jerk about the party," I said, leaning back against my headboard. "I mean, for not helping and all that stuff. I realized that you were right. I have been spending a lot of time with Jake, and I haven't been paying much attention to . . . you know . . . to you."

"It's okay," Ashley said. "I understand that Jake is really important to you right now. I didn't mean to be so critical." She sighed and shifted her position, crossing her legs and bringing her knees up

118

under her chin. "I'm really happy for you, Mary-Kate."

"Can we just never fight again?" I smiled.

Ashley broke into a wide grin. "Sounds good to me."

She reached out and wrapped her arms around me, and I hugged her back, hard. It felt so good to have all of that dread and guilt and misery hugged away!

"So?" I said. "Tell me about your date!"

Ashley glanced down at her hands. "Mom and Dad told you about that, huh?"

"Well, of course they did!" I answered. "It was totally weird. They kinda had to fill me in."

"Remember that mystery guy from Todd's party? His name is Ben Jones," Ashley explained. "He's in my Driver's Ed class and he's soooo cute. Mary-Kate, you'd really like him. He has this amazing sense of humor, and . . ."

She trailed off and stared at some far point over my head, all dreamy-eyed.

"And what?" I asked. "What?"

"And he's the best kisser ever." Ashley sighed.

"He *kissed* you?" I blurted.

"Yeah." She nodded absently.

For a second there I thought she was going to float off into the clouds.

"Wow," I said. "This is pretty serious."

"I guess so," Ashley agreed. She shrugged and leaned back beside me, her head propped up on a couple of my throw pillows.

"I'm really comfortable with him," she told me. "He's a great guy."

I scooted down so that I was closer to her. "I'm really happy for you, Ashley," I said. "I can't believe we both met such amazing guys at practically the same time. It's almost as if it was meant to be or something."

"Yeah, it is," Ashley said.

"So?" I patted her arm in the silly, excited way Mom always did when she wanted news from us. "When do I get to meet him?"

Ashley turned onto her side and propped her head up on her hand. "That's something I wanted to talk to you about," she said. "How would you feel about having a boy-girl party after all?"

If I could have screamed without waking up my parents, I would have. Instead, I jumped out of bed—and almost tripped doing it.

"Are you kidding me?" I glared at Ashley.

"What?" Ashley asked, sitting up straight. "I thought you'd be happy. Isn't that what you wanted?"

I felt like I was going to explode from frustration. "Yes! That was what I *wanted*!" I pushed my hands into my hair and held it back from my face. "But, Ashley, after our fight I un-invited Jake."

"Well, then all you have to do is re-invite him the next time you see him," Ashley said. "He'll be psyched and we'll get to have a guy-girl party. See? Everyone wins!"

I sighed and closed my eyes, telling myself to breathe. Then I sat down on my bed again and stared up at the ceiling.

"You're right," I answered slowly. "I'll just re-invite him and everything will be fine—once Jake gets over the fact that I'm a total nutball."

Ashley was quiet for a couple of moments. Then she sighed. "Remember the other day when we were talking about what it was going to be like to be sixteen?"

"Yeah. Parties . . . driving . . . clothes . . . boys," I said.

"Well, I'm starting to think it's not going to be that simple," Ashley said. "I always figured we'd be doing all that stuff together."

"But we're not," I finished. "We're not driving together or going to parties together . . . and the guys we like even go to completely different schools."

"Exactly." Ashley's eyes narrowed with concern. "What if turning sixteen means we're going to grow apart?"

My stomach tightened. "Well, we won't let it," I said, determined.

"How can we not?" Ashley asked.

"We'll make a pact," I said. Ashley laughed and rolled her eyes, but I was dead serious. "I mean it! We'll say we both understand that we might be doing a lot of things without each other, but no matter what, we'll always be there for each other and we'll always be best friends."

"Sounds good to me." Ashley smiled.

After not talking to Ashley for two days, this conversation was like heaven. Everything was going to be fine between Ashley and me. And I would talk to Jake and make him understand. We'd invite the guys and we'd have the most amazing sweet sixteen party ever.

Everything's going to be fine now, I thought. *Absolutely, totally fine.*

chapter fourteen

Monday afternoon I walked into the cafeteria and spotted Jake at the front of the lunch line, digging in his pocket for his wallet as he balanced his tray with his free hand.

"It's now or never," I coached myself.

I rolled my shoulders back, ignoring the nervous knots in my stomach, and weaved my way through the crowd.

"Jake!" I called.

He looked up, and his face turned grim. Then he walked off in the other direction, heading for the window wall. My stomach tightened as he slid his way along the windows to get to his table. There was almost no space over there, so he was basically taking the most difficult route to his table. Was it just to get away from me?

I intercepted Jake before he could get to his friends. He stopped short, sighing impatiently.

"Jake, what's wrong?" I asked. "I tried to call you all weekend."

"Yeah, well, I was busy," he mumbled.

"I . . . uh . . . I need to talk to you." I started to play with the rings on my right hand, twisting them around and around my fingers.

"Sorry. I have to go," Jake said.

He took a step forward, forcing me out of his way, and walked off toward his table without looking back.

My heart was pounding like crazy as I watched him go. What happened? Jake and I had a great time last week. Why was he suddenly treating me like he didn't care about me?

Hot tears pricked at the corners of my eyes. I hurried to the bathroom so no one would see me cry.

"Oh my gosh, Mary-Kate! Are you okay?" Lauren blurted when she saw me. She and Brittany had found me in the library after lunch.

"You're all puffy!" Brittany whispered, handing me a couple of tissues from her bag. "What happened? Where were you at lunch?"

"In the bathroom," I told her, wiping my eyes. "I tried to talk to Jake, but he wouldn't even *look* at me." My heart sank all over again. "He just . . . *dismissed* me."

"Why?" Lauren asked, her forehead wrinkling. "Did you have a fight?"

"No!" I said, loudly enough to earn a "Shhh!" from the librarian at the front of the room. "That's the thing. Everything was fine on Friday."

"What a jerk!" Brittany slumped back in her chair. "You don't need a guy who's going to treat you like that, Mary-Kate."

I sighed miserably. Jake wasn't a jerk. At least, he never had been before. I wished I could figure out what had set him off.

"Are you sure you didn't do *anything*?" Lauren asked.

"The only thing I can think of is the conversation we had on Friday about the party." I pulled my bookbag toward me and rested my chin on it.

"Oh, so you did un-invite him?" Lauren asked.

"Yeah, but he was totally cool about it. He said he understood," I explained. "Now he won't even talk to me!"

The second bell rang, and Todd Malone slipped through the library door. I felt a quick surge of hope. Todd was friends with Jake. Maybe he'd know what was going on.

"Todd!" I whispered as he started toward the periodical section. I waved him over to our table.

"Hi, guys," he said. "I guess you want to talk about Jake, huh?"

"Do you know what's going on?" I asked.

"Yep," Todd said. I could tell by the strained look on his face that he didn't want to be in the middle of this, but I didn't know where else to turn. He lowered himself into the free chair at our table. "I was there when it happened."

"What are you talking about?" I demanded.

"Here's the deal," Todd said. "The other day I went to the park with John Lee and my friend Ben, from Harrison. Jake was already there shooting hoops, so we decided to play two on two."

"Okay," I said.

"So we're playing and Jake and Ben get to talking and pretty soon they both realized that they were dating twin sisters," Todd explained.

"Wait—Ben from Harrison is Ashley's Ben?" Brittany asked.

"Right," Todd said. "So then Ben asks Jake if he's going to your sweet sixteen and Jake says 'No, it's an all-girl party' and Ben gets all confused because Ashley had just invited him the night before and then—"

"And then Jake went ballistic." My stomach flipped over.

"Well, Jake doesn't ever really go ballistic," Todd said. "But he did get quiet, and he left pretty soon after that."

I felt sick. This couldn't be happening.

"I still don't get it," Lauren whispered. "Why is Jake mad at you?"

"Because he thinks I lied," I said flatly. "When he found out Ben was invited to the sweet sixteen, he figured I lied when I told him it was an all-girl party. He probably thinks I just didn't want him to come so I made up the all-girl thing as an excuse."

"Wow," Brittany said. "No wonder he's mad."

"Well, you're just going to have to explain it to him," Lauren declared. "Tell him what really happened."

"Right," I replied. "If he'll ever talk to me again."

"This is a nightmare," Mary-Kate said after she explained what had happened with Jake. She flopped back on my bed and stared up at the ceiling.

"Listen, we can fix this," I said, clicking into organization mode. "You'll talk to Jake in the next few days. He's hurt right now, but he has to listen to you eventually. You'll explain everything, and he'll be fine."

"Do you really think so?" Mary-Kate asked hopefully.

"Yes," I told her. "Then, all we have to do is call Wilson, and tell him not to send out any of the invitations. We'll cut half the girls from our list, add a few boys, and—ta-da!—problem solved!"

Just having a plan made me feel better. I grabbed the phone to dial Wilson's number, but it rang in my hand. I jumped at the sound, then answered.

"Ashley? Hi, it's Wilson!" the voice on the line said.

"Wilson! I was just about to call you. There are some things about the party that Mary-Kate and I need to discuss with you."

"Great!" Wilson said. "But before you get into that, I have good news. I flew back from Aspen a day early so I got your invitations out in the mail today!"

Uh-oh. A lump formed in my throat.

"Ashley? What's wrong?" Mary-Kate asked when she noticed my expression.

I told Wilson I'd call him back, and hung up the phone.

"Mary-Kate, we've got trouble," I told my sister. "Wilson already sent out the invitations!"

My sister looked ill. "You mean, we're stuck having an all-girl party?"

"Not if we act fast." I grabbed a jacket from my closet. "Come on, Mary-Kate. We have to find a way to get those invitations back!"

**The countdown to
the biggest party of the year continues!
Find out what happens next in**

Book 2:
Wishes and Dreams

Ashley and I were walking down the hallway at the end of lunch period when we ran into Melanie Han and Tashema Mitchell.

"Hey, you guys! We're *so* excited about your party!" Melanie said.

"Sending updates about your sweet sixteen by e-mail is so cool. How'd you come up with that idea?" Tashema asked.

"Oh, it just, um—came to us," I said.

My sister and I exchanged a look. No one knew that the location of our sweet sixteen was a secret—because *we* didn't even know where we were having it! There were fourteen days and counting until our big party and we still hadn't found the perfect party place!

But that was okay. I knew that Ashley and I

would come up with something awesome—even if we did it with seconds to spare.

"So when's the next update?" Melanie asked.

"Soon," Ashley teased. "But we can't tell you when, because that would ruin the surprise."

"Can't you give us a clue? A teensy tiny clue?" Melanie begged.

"Not even one," I told her. "Just keep checking your e-mail."

"Okay, but the suspense is killing me," Tashema said before she and Melanie walked off.

I nudged Ashley with my elbow. "Sounds like our plan is working great!"

Ashley smiled. "You're right. No one suspects a thing!"

We turned the corner at the end of the hall— and nearly crashed into Rachel Adams.

"Hey, Mary-Kate. Hi, Ashley. I got your e-mail invitation—thanks!" she said.

"You're welcome," I told her with a smile. "Do you think you can make it to our party?"

"I'll be there for sure—and I *love* that the girls are inviting the guys. I'm asking tons of boys, so we should have enough to dance with and—"

I turned and looked at Ashley, whose face had gone completely pale. "Um, did you just say you're inviting *tons* of boys?" I asked Rachel. "You were only supposed to invite one."

Rachel looked at me with a confused expression. "Well, your e-mail said to invite *guys*. Plural," she explained. "So I thought I'd invite the guys' basketball team. Then asked my older brother if he'd come along and bring a couple of his friends, because some of them are really cute."

"Yeah, um, that sounds great!" Ashley said. She started pulling me away. "I'm sorry, Rachel, but we have to run now. See you later!"

Ashley and I raced down the hall. I knew where we were headed. We had to get to the computer lab to check out the e-mail we sent.

"We didn't," I said as we ran.

"We couldn't have," Ashley agreed. We raced into the lab and grabbed a seat at one of the terminals. Ashley signed on to our e-mail account in record time. She pulled up our "Sent Mail."

Suddenly, there it was on the screen: our latest e-mail update about our sweet sixteen party. Ashley ran her finger along the message until she got to the important line:

"Please invite the guys of your choice," she read.

"Rachel was right! It's *guys*—plural!" I wailed.

Several heads popped up from behind computer monitors as people strained to see what was going on.

"Mary-Kate," Ashley whispered, "the entire school is going to come to our party now. The entire city! We can't have a party for all those people. What are we going to do?

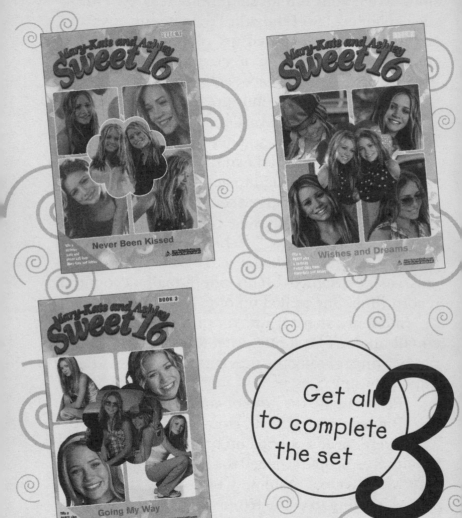

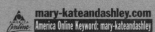

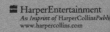

Celebrate your birthday with Mary-Kate and Ashley!

Enter below for your chance to win a birthday party for you and 10 friends!

Watch your favorite Mary-Kate and Ashley movies with your friends on your very own brand-new TV/VCR combination unit. Then, it's time for your birthday party which includes; party food, birthday cake, and the following gifts to share with your friends:

- 11 Mary-Kate and Ashley videos
- 11 Autographed Mary-Kate and Ashley books
- 11 Mary-Kate and Ashley video games
- 11 Mary-Kate and Ashley music CDs

You'll even get a personal phone call from Mary-Kate and Ashley!*

*(At a time to be arranged)

MARY-KATE AND ASHLEY SWEET 16
Birthday Party Sweepstakes

OFFICIAL RULES:

1. No purchase necessary.

2. To enter complete the official entry form or hand print your name, address, age, and phone number along with the words "MARY-KATE AND ASHLEY SWEET 16 Birthday Party Sweepstakes" on a 3" x 5" card and mail to: MARY-KATE AND ASHLEY SWEET 16 Birthday Party Sweepstakes, c/o HarperEntertainment, Attn: Children's Marketing Department, 10 East 53rd Street, New York, NY 10022. Entries must be received **no later than August 31, 2002.** Enter as often as you wish, but each entry must be mailed separately. One entry per envelope. Partially completed, illegible, or mechanically reproduced entries will not be accepted. Sponsors are not responsible for lost, late, mutilated, illegible, stolen, postage due, incomplete, or misdirected entries. All entries become the property of Dualstar Entertainment Group, Inc., and will not be returned.

3. Sweepstakes open to all legal residents of the United States (excluding Colorado and Rhode Island), who are between the ages of five and fifteen by August 31, 2002, excluding employees and immediate family members of HarperCollins Publishers, Inc., ("HarperCollins"), Parachute Properties and Parachute Press, Inc., and their respective subsidiaries and affiliates, officers, directors, shareholders, employees, agents, attorneys, and other representatives (individually and collectively "Parachute"), Dualstar Entertainment Group, Inc., and its subsidiaries and affiliates, officers, directors, shareholders, employees, agents, attorneys, and other representatives (individually and collectively "Dualstar"), and their respective parent companies, affiliates, subsidiaries, advertising, promotion and fulfillment agencies, and the persons with whom each of the above are domiciled. Offer void where prohibited or restricted by law.

4. Odds of winning depend on the total number of entries received. Approximately 675,000 sweepstakes announcements published. All prizes will be awarded. Winners will be randomly drawn on or about September 15, 2002, by HarperCollins, whose decisions are final. Potential winner will be notified by mail and will be required to sign and return an affidavit of eligibility and release of liability within 14 days of notification. Prizes won by minors will be awarded to parent or legal guardian who must sign and return all required legal documents. By acceptance of the prize, winner consents to the use of his or her name, photograph, likeness, and personal information by HarperCollins, Parachute, Dualstar, and for publicity purposes without further compensation except where prohibited.

5. One (1) **Grand Prize Winner** wins a birthday party for the winner and 10 friends which consists of the following: a TV/VCR combination unit, food (including pizza, soda, birthday cake), party decorations (including streamers, balloons), 11 MARY-KATE AND ASHLEY videos, 11 autographed MARY-KATE AND ASHLEY books, 11 MARY-KATE AND ASHLEY music CDs, and 11 MARY-KATE AND ASHLEY video games; In addition, Grand Prize winner will receive a phone call from Mary-Kate and Ashley at a time to be arranged. Approximate retail value $1,500.00.

6. Only one prize will be awarded per individual, family, or household. Prizes are non-transferable and cannot be sold or redeemed for cash. No cash substitute is available. Any federal, state, or local taxes are the responsibility of the winner. Sponsor may substitute prize of equal or greater value, if necessary, due to availability.

7. Additional terms: By participating, entrants agree a) to the official rules and decisions of the judges, which will be final in all respects; and to waive any claim to ambiguity of the official rules and b) to release, discharge, and hold harmless HarperCollins, Parachute, Dualstar, and their affiliates, subsidiaries, and advertising and promotion agencies from and against any and all liability or damages associated with acceptance, use, or misuse of any prize received in this sweepstakes.

8. Any dispute arising from this Sweepstakes will be determined according to the laws of the State of New York, without reference to its conflict of law principles, and the entrants consent to the personal jurisdiction of the State and Federal courts located in New York County and agree that such courts have exclusive jurisdiction over all such disputes.

9. To obtain the name of the winners, please send your request and a self-addressed stamped envelope (excluding residents of Vermont and Washington) to MARY-KATE AND ASHLEY SWEET 16 Birthday Party Sweepstakes, c/o HarperEntertainment, Attn: Children's Marketing Department, 10 East 53rd Street, New York, NY 10022 by October 1, 2002. Sweepstakes Sponsor: HarperCollins Publishers, Inc.

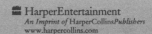

The Ultimate Fa...

mary-kate

Don't miss

📖 HarperEntertainment
An Imprint of HarperCollinsPublishers
www.harpercollins.com

 mary-kateandashley.com
America Online Keyword: mary-kateandashley

 DUALSTAR
PUBLICATIONS

Books created and produced by Parachute Publishing, L.L.C., in cooperation with Dualstar Publications, a division of Dualstar Entertainment Group, Inc.
TWO OF A KIND © 2001 Warner Bros. THE NEW ADVENTURES OF MARY-KATE & ASHLEY and STARRING IN TM & © 2001 Dualstar Entertainment Group, Inc.